W9-BUP-876

STIGMATA

STIGMATA

Phyllis Alesia Perry

HYPERION

New York

Library of Congress Cataloging-in-Publication Data

Perry, Phyllis Alesia.
    Stigmata / Phyllis Alesia Perry. — 1st ed.
        p.   cm.
    ISBN 0-7868-6408-7
    1. Afro-Americans—Fiction.   I. Title
PS3566.E7135S75   1998
813' .54—dc21   98–5324
                                                     CIP

Designed by *Gloria Adelson / LuLu Graphics*

FIRST EDITION

10 9 8 7 6 5 4 3 2 1

For Arcola Johnson Perry
and her sisters

There is a certain place in Alabama, which I love too much to name, where stories seem to bubble up from the ground. I'm so grateful that my blood flows from that place and much of what I do is in remembrance of all the people who loved me there. I don't ever want to imagine my life without the love of that family and the friends who have surprised and humbled me with their faith and support. Of those, I'd like to especially thank:

My mother, Arcola Johnson Perry, for trusting my vision and always letting me be my flighty, crazy, dreamy self; the agent, John McGregor, my buddy, my advocate, my task-master; my grandmother and guardian angel, Arcola Barr Johnson; Leigh Haber, for believing that there's room in the world for the words we both love; the girls who got my back—Valerie Boyd, Thonnia Lee, and Sharon Rowell; Penelope and Trellis Price-Gladney, who never say no; my equipment manager and pep rally leader, E. Lynn Harris; and all those other cheerleaders along the way who kept me from dropping out of the game, including Kieth L. Thomas, Ricky Carson, and Cory Smith.

Ayo (Bessie Ward)
(1832?–1900) ∞

Samuel
(1852–1918)

Peak
(1853–60)

Ben
(1858–78)

Grace ∞ George Lancaster
(1900–58)   (1900–70)

Mary Nell ∞
(1902–74)

Frank ∞ Alene Ranson
(1924)   (1928)

Phillip
(1924)

Gray ∞ Roberta Craig
(1948)   (1952)

Billie
(1944)

James ∞ Beatrice Ames
(1922–63)   (1938)

Ruth
(1961)

Samuel Ward
(1813–70)

Lemuel
(1860–1935)

Joy ⚭ Frank Mobley
(1869–1942)   (1866–1940)

Henry Evans
(1899–1959)

Eva ⚭ Adam Davidson
(1908)   (1907–1968)

Sarah ⚭ Dr. John Daniel DuBose
(1934)   (1934)

Eddie
(1950–69)

Elizabeth Joyce (Lizzie)
(1960)

Patricia ⚭ John Taylor
(1923)   (1924)

John Jr.
(1944)

I guess it is the contrast that makes me laugh.

In the two years I've been here, it never struck me before today how plush the room is. I come in before Dr. Harper and take my usual seat on the purple sofa flanked by two purple armchairs and punctuated with a round, glass coffee table. I've never been alone in here, and, without the distraction of conversation and analysis, it's easy to sink, smiling, into the softness of the room. Outside the door to the office, which the doctor doesn't call an office, but his "place" ("Come on down to my place, Lizzie, when you finish in the game room, so we can talk."), everyone speaks in quiet, unhurried tones. Well, despite the shine and the softness, it is a nuthouse. A padded cell.

As I drop onto the lush cushions of the sofa and take a sip from the cup of herbal tea that the doctor's assistant hands me

at the door, I'm acutely aware of having made it to the end. I'm
at the end of the pain and the yelling, the crying and the cring-
ing. The voices no longer hound me. My world is neat and un-
stained. There is no more blood, but there are scars.

I recall the beginning, long ago and far removed from here,
when the world was bloody, when the walls and beds were
hard and so were the doctors.

Before I learned to lie.

"Ohh-kaay," I hear Harper say as the door opens. He sweeps
into the office, carrying files and looking delicious in jeans and
a black polo shirt. He thinks he looks like a college student, but
I've looked enough psychiatrists in the face to know one when
I see one. Pretty brown skin, white teeth and practiced charm
do nothing to disguise that certain note in a shrink's voice that
says, "You're crazy and I'm not."

"I'm sorry to get here so late, Lizzie," he says, tucking a thick
file under his arm and throwing the rest on his nearby desk. He
drops into one of the chairs. "I just have to do this last session
for the record."

He smiles at me. "You're all clear to leave, but I want to have
this last session down."

"Of course," I reply. I like the guy fine, but he's still annoying. Does he know? I pluck at the pocket of my white shirt. I rub
my fingers over the raised scars on my wrists.

"Are you nervous about going back to your parents?" he
asks, his eyes on my hands moving on my skin.

"Well, yeah. What do you think?"

"Do you think they're afraid?"

"Yeah."

"How are you going to handle their fear of you?"

"I'll just have to convince them . . . let them know I don't . . . ah . . . won't . . . hurt myself anymore. That I know better now what's really happening."

"You admit then, that it was a rather elaborate delusion?"

"Umm, yes." I laugh softly. "But these things happen."

"Not to everybody. That's why they're afraid."

I nod but say nothing.

"What's your name?"

Startled by his question, I smile nervously, showing the bare minimum of tooth enamel. "I've been in here two years and now you don't know my name? That's funny, Harper."

"Humor me." His head is down as he scribbles something in the file open on his lap. The paper inside is thick enough to form a stable writing surface.

"Elizabeth DuBose. Elizabeth Joyce DuBose."

"I've heard about you. Your mother calls you Lizzie. You tried to commit suicide."

"It was a long time ago."

"But it *was* a suicide attempt, not something else?"

"Oh, I see." I lift my brow. "A little test. OK. Yes, I did try to . . . make an exit, you might say. I was twenty. Having bad dreams about my long-dead relatives, that sort of thing. I had been having them for . . . let's see . . . since I was fourteen."

He leans forward in the chair, that easy smile gone, his hands cupping his chin. The elbow he has propped on the file slips, loosening something that falls on the carpet. As he bends to pick it up, his gaze never leaves my face. His eyes are wide, like a kid around a campfire listening to ghost stories. I glimpse the

photograph he tucks back between some papers. Bloody bandages. Wild eyes.

"What happened when you were fourteen?" he continues.

"I inherited something . . ."

"A diary?"

"Yes, my great-grandmother's . . ."

"And something else?"

"A . . . quilt. That belonged to my grandmother." Harper's
face swims in front of me, blurring a little, and I see colors run
towards each other and make those familiar faces sewn so carefully that they talk across the surface of fading cloth. I flex my
fingers and then ball them into fists. I see Harper looking at
my hands. He notices everything.

"And . . . ? What was it about this diary and this quilt that got
you so wound up?" He leans even closer, which hardly seems
possible, not letting me go with those eyes. Damn the man for
being so fine. He is so close I can't concentrate on my obses-
sions—the quilt, the scars, everything. God. I haven't had sex
since the last decade. I'd probably tell him what he wanted to
hear even if I hadn't already gathered up the lies necessary for
my escape.

Used to be, I wondered why it was him and not all the others who really got to me, made me want to get up, finally, and
go away from this place. Maybe because he was black and a
man—I would never claim to be above all that. Something
about him—glowing eyes, quick smile, slow, steady conversation and endless cups of tea—reminds me of life at its most
mundane, everything I miss. He is the most unclinical clinician
I've ever met, though I still recognize his medical degree underneath all that familiarity.

But there are other reasons.

Mostly, I am through with silence, don't need it anymore. I've polished my story of redemption and restored mental health—the one responsible for my impending freedom—to such a high shine that I've dazzled Harper and everyone else.

"I really believed it, you know," I whisper to him now, in as tense a voice as I can manage without choking on a giggle. "The pictures there on that quilt were like some long-faded memory to me. You understand? I was a teenager, that quilt was decades old; but I could remember sewing it, I could remember folding it. And all the stories became true." I throw his stare back at him. "How come mystics can talk about reincarnation all day long and I get committed for it?"

"Because of this." He grasps my wrists and encircles the scar tissue with his fingers. He's touching me. Do his superiors know he's touching me? "And that . . ." He points at the circles of raised flesh around my ankles. "Those aren't from chains and manacles, are they, Lizzie?"

"No," I croak. I smell the air coming through his office window from outside the hospital's brick walls, and despite the familiar fragrance of Atlanta summer smog, I like it. It smells like freedom to me.

Harper won't let go. "Where did these scars come from?" he asks.

I take in a big gulp of air, dismayed now at how hard it is to get the words out. "Me," I say. "They came from me. I used a paring knife. Confusion makes you do things like that. All I could think about was the woman in the pictures, the one on the quilt, and what she must have gone through. I lost myself there, for a long time. But . . . I'm all right now. I just want to go home."

He releases my arms and shifts in the seat, relaxing against the purple cushions.

"And you will. You done good. It's finally over, at least this part is." He writes something in the fat file and then gets up to throw it on top of the other folders on his desk.

I laugh a little, but only on the inside; outwardly, I am drawn up tight, quiet. He is so sure he's cured my madness. There'll probably be a best-seller soon, the kind of book where the author's name is bigger than the title. And after I am back home in Tuskegee, curled up on Mother's good sofa drinking her good wine, I'll turn on the TV and he'll be there, flirting with Oprah.

Poor guy. He doesn't know there is no cure for what I've got.

Outside the office, I lean against the wall for a moment, just getting used to the idea of home, of going back to where the pain began, but with tougher skin this time.

And all it took was fourteen years and some well-acted moments of sanity.

Words last heard on the schoolyard at Our Lady of Mercy Catholic school keep running through my head. I actually mouth them as I walk to my room to finish packing.

Ah hah. I fooled you. I fooled you.

December 26, 1898

Mama dont move round much these days. She sits and sews. Christmas fine Frank ate a lot and Sam was here with his wife and young uns and Mama make a big fuss over them but after they went home on down the road she sat for a long time lookin after them out the window. Then she with Jim Beam. She can't sleep either. I have never seen Aunt Eva without her sister Mary Nell, and what is left of Mary Nell rides the ivory pillow in a super-deluxe casket at Danvers Funeral Home, waiting for that last journey.

You know how sometimes when you're just about to fall asleep and sounds grow around you and maybe, just maybe, you hear your name floating by? Every time my eyes close, I feel an exhale of hot air brush my cheek and my lids fly open and I wonder about Aunt Mary Nell's last words.

She was my great-aunt really, my grandmother's sister. In the death room is a hazy, dream-like photograph of the three of them—Eva, Mary Nell and my grandmother, Grace—standing on the front porch of a house. They were young then, teenagers in love with the camera, looking vibrant even in that fading old picture, an image from the other end of time. They wear identical high-pile hairdos with hats, dazzling white dresses and black lace-up boots. They hold their white-gloved hands in various la-de-da poses ("Oh, yes," said Aunt Eva once. "It was Easter. First new clothes we'd had in three or four years. Storebought, too. And we worked for days on that hair. A tornado couldn't move it.").

Grace, my mother Sarah's mother, is on the right, one hand on her hip, the other placed languidly against her long neck. But there is nothing posed about the way she holds up her chin and looks into the camera, eyes straight ahead and challenging.

Grace packed a trunk and left Johnson Creek in 1940 and was never seen alive by her family again. Forty years old, settled, from an old family. And then she hopped a train and was gone. To the folk of Johnson Creek, she will always be the church matron who just up and walked away from her husband and three children. A respectable woman disgraced is enough to provide juicy talk for decades. So by the time Grace died in 1958, before I was born, her legend was already well established. She never came back, but the trunk did—in 1945—accompanied by a mysterious letter to Mary Nell.

I never stop pestering Aunt Mary Nell about that letter and that trunk.

When I was younger, the end of the school year in Tuskegee would find my cousin Ruth Evans and I being packed up and shipped out to Johnson Creek to be deposited at Eva and Mary Nell's house. Mary Nell was Ruth's paternal grandmother.

Ruth and I often sat in the hall of the house at Johnson Creek long after we were supposed to be in bed, listening to Eva and Mary Nell talk, and Grace's funeral was one of their favorite subjects. There were folks who still believed the rumor that Grace had run away with some jackleg preacher man who caught her eye, but Mary Nell and Eva apparently knew better. They always rolled their eyes and shook their heads whenever that story surfaced.

They told the story the same way every time: First came the telegram from some man they didn't know and then the body to Union Springs. When the hearse arrived in Johnson Creek, everybody turned out to see the infamous woman who had abandoned her husband, George, and their children to run away "up the country somewhere."

"Grace sho' gave 'em a show," Aunt Eva would say, smiling. "They couldn't believe that fancy casket and all. And the singing and music she ordered . . . ! They still whispering round here 'bout how she made her money up north. And how she bought that land down here and set George and the children up real fine . . . oh, they was just green . . ."

"Poor George," Mary Nell would say. "He didn't know whether to play the grieving widower, the outraged husband or the lord of the manor."

Then she would laugh until she snorted.

Speculating on the contents of the trunk was a never-ending game. Ruth and I invented elaborate stories about things we'd never seen, things that probably didn't exist. We didn't even know where the key was. The aunts often found us in Mary Nell's room fiddling with the trunk's old-fashioned, slightly rusting padlock. I think we hoped the thing would just fall apart in our hands and finally the contents of the magic box would be there before us. We were sure it held undreamed-of treasures.

Mary Nell would come into the room and look at us with wistful sadness before telling us to leave it alone. Their reticence about the trunk was strange to me because the two of them usually greeted almost every other thing we did—every exuberant prank and escapade—with loud laughter. But when I asked about the trunk, I was told: "You too young for that. You not ready yet."

"I am ready," I would say. When I was smaller, I always said this to a tummy or chest and Eva or Mary Nell would just hug me real hard and give me some chore to do. Lately, I'd been looking them both dead in the eyes. "I am ready," I said only a month ago while visiting with my mother, Sarah. I had straightened my back and, trying to project all the maturity of my fourteen years, locked onto Mary Nell's soft gaze and said, "Grandmama is dead. Why can't I read the letter? Why can't I look in the trunk?"

Mary Nell just shook her head and muttered, "Getting tall as Grace."

I never did get to sleep.

I stand blinking in the sun at Mary Nell's graveside, not far from where Grace is buried. I try to imagine the two of them giggling together now, though Mary Nell's boom of a laugh had become little more than a wistful smile by the time last year's stroke got through with her. She always seemed to expect another one after that.

"Seventy-two years is enough time for anyone, I suppose," she told me during that last visit. She was out on the porch slowly scooping dirt into clay pots for her geraniums. I resisted the urge to offer my help and just watched her loosely held trowel sink inch by inch into the tin bucket of soil. Most of the dirt ended up on the rough-planked boards of the porch, some of it slipping through the cracks; I could see Eva's gray cat sitting underneath the porch watching it pile up with growing fascination. Used to be, an excruciatingly neat Mary Nell would have swept up the mess right away. But that was last year, and she no longer had time to stop going about her business.

"Aunt Mary Nell," I said that day, flashing my sunniest smile. "You'll be out here kicking up a fuss when you're a hundred."

"No. I ready, I 'spect, to get on with it," she answered, holding up a geranium plant and shaking the roots. "Can't remember what color this blooms. Deep pink, I think. Just the color for summer."

A month later she died just as she was waking to a late-spring dawn. Massive stroke. Aunt Eva went into her room and found her there, sleepy-eyed and looking off in the distance at something no one else could see.

"She had been dreaming," Eva said later, without elaboration.

After the funeral is finished and Aunt Mary Nell laid down and the sticky red dirt smoothed over, after the steady parade of kinfolk and just-like-kinfolk have cried and giggled into their fried chicken, potato salad and chocolate cake and then slowly drifted out, Aunt Eva's neighbor Son Jackson brings a large leather trunk out to the porch.

Ruth and her mother, Beatrice, come out of the house behind him, and Mother, who's standing there in the front yard leaning her short frame against my father's tall one, stops dabbing at her damp eyes to straighten and stare.

"Is that . . . ?" She looks at Aunt Eva, who nods and says, "Grace's."

Mother has already taken a step towards the trunk when Aunt Eva says, looking at Mother, but speaking to me, "Mary Nell was keeping it for you, Lizzie. She told me before she passed that she thought you were the right age for this." She turns away from my mother's stricken face and hands me a rusty key and a crumpled, aging letter. Dated 1945.

"She . . . " Mother pulls at the brim of her black, lace-draped hat, her lips knotted into a frown, her eyes still puffy from crying at the gravesite. "Why . . . ? Mama died before Lizzie was even born."

"Can't really answer that, baby," says Aunt Eva softly. "But she says in the letter to give it to her granddaughter."

Mother lowers her chin; the hat hides her eyes. I see Daddy come up behind her and wrap his large hand around hers.

He puts Grace's trunk in the back of the Buick and we go

home to Tuskegee. All the way, I watch the back of Mother's head atop her ramrod-rigid spine. I know she has never seen the inside of the trunk. I know she is thinking about Grace's letter. I ask her if she's OK and she just mumbles at me.

After we get back and Daddy dumps Grace's trunk on the living room floor, he retreats to his study and Mother and I stand on either side of it. I don't know what to say to her, and for a few heartbeats she doesn't move at all. Then she says, her voice so tight that the words barely make it past her lips, "I'm so tired; we'll deal with it in the morning."

I try, I really try to wait. I'm in bed an hour or so later when I hear my parents in their bedroom talking. Soon their voices fade and there is, it seems, just me and the night.

The dark nestles in; it lies close to my face and perches on my young bones as I turn over and over against the sheets in the high iron bed. Might as well be back on Aunt Eva's couch.

No sleep. And that is the start of things. Because if you don't sleep, you think and have conversations with yourself that, in the morning, are startling.

In the quiet night, the trunk is all I think about. Ruth and I had talked about that unopened trunk for years. How was I going to wait until morning? I turn on the lamp and reach under my pillow, where I'd stuck my grandmother's letter. It is postmarked Detroit. The elegant handwriting is familiar.

Dearest Mary Nell,
 The strangeness has dogged me north and I know to learn all I can about past days.
 I took Mama's papers with me as you said I should, hope they would help me sort things out and they have. It pains

me that I missed Mama's funeral but I had a sickness on me at that time that would not let me travel. I send the papers back to you with the other things. Things that belong with the family. I also have sent that quilt I was working on when I left. It's finished and Ayo's whole story is set on it. I feel better now it's through. No telling where I might end up so it be safer with you.

Now Mary please do not show these to my baby girl Sarah. Well I reckon she aint such a baby no more. She will ask questions that you cannot answer that I'm not sure I can answer. And I could never burden her with the thought that her mother is crazy. I could not curse her with these things that are happening to me. I thought getting all that down on the quilt in front of me out of me would get rid of it somehow. I don't know about that. But I know I can't pass it on to her this craziness. So save it but not for Sarah. Maybe Sarah will be safe.

I feel that others after us will need to know. Our grands maybe will need to get these things. Please leave these for my granddaughter. I know she aint here yet. But I have faith that you and Eva will know when the time is right and when it is she will be waiting.

Please don't worry. I am well. Somehow it is all easier to bear without being around the pity of your loved ones but it is harder too. My poor George would have done something about it. I am glad I saved him the trouble.

Kiss Eva and Sarah and my twin boys for me.

Your sister,

Grace

I slide the letter under the pillow, flick off the light. The trunk sits in the dark, and my conversation with myself searches for all the reasons one has to wait until morning for everything. But there is no reason, and I throw the covers off to search for my robe.

Tiptoeing down the dim hall, I stumble into the living room. The trunk is squarely where Daddy left it, in the center of the floor. I go on to the kitchen, to the drawer where there is a large flashlight. Mystery, I think, as I flick it on. I like this. Maybe I've read too much Nancy Drew. I think there is one called *The Secret of the Old Trunk* or something. Only in a bona fide Nancy Drew Mystery, Nancy would find the trunk in a creepy, dusty basement, not at the end of a funeral. Nobody dies in Nancy Drew.

It is mere leather bound by wood, cracking in places, but I kneel before the trunk as if before an altar. The metal loops holding the lock have rusted and there, just under my beam of light, I see that a spider has made her dream home.

I've left the key in the lock and I turn it, opening the lid; an old smell, a sigh, a breath escapes from the past. But when I stick my light in, I see no treasure, just a stack of papers. None of Grace's imagined riches rediscovered. Paper.

A sheaf of it clings together, tied with ancient string. As I try to slide the string off, bits of paper crumble, becoming dust as I watch. I bite my lower lip and put the papers aside. There are other, official-looking papers in there too and, underneath, two shoe boxes and something that looks like cloth.

Inside one of the boxes there is jewelry—necklaces and brooches—as well as gloves and handkerchiefs edged with crocheted lace. Now this is more like it. Treasures. Old treasures, from the looks of things.

I lift one glove to my face and inhale: dust and, very briefly, lavender. Sneezing, I put it back and open the other box, which

contains two well-worn leather pouches. One of these holds
two stones and a very old bit of blue cloth. In the other, there is
a small doll made of grass and sticks.

The doll falls apart in my hands, so I quickly put it back in the
pouch, which, in turn, goes back into the shoe box.

I shine the flashlight on the sheaf of papers. The writing
seems centuries old. I hold the light as close as I can to the surface of the yellow paper, trying to read without removing the
string that ties it together. I don't understand any of it. Something about eternity.

*We are forever. Here at the bottom of heaven we live in the circle. We
back and gone and back again.*

I am Ayo. Joy. I choose to remember.

*This is for those whose bones lie in the heart of mother ocean for
those who tomorrows I never knew who groaned and died in the damp
dark beside me. You rite this daughter for me and for them.*

I hear a click, the shuffle of feet. Daddy, probably, on the way
to the toilet. Off with the flashlight, the paper stuffed back into
the trunk, the lid snapped down and shut. I go and crouch behind the sofa.

Small feet pad down the hall and I see a silhouette in the living room doorway. Not Daddy, though.

Mother comes in rather tentatively and I hold my breath. She
puts her arms out in front of her, groping. I see their shadows
in the weak light from the hall, stretching towards the dining
room. When she goes into the kitchen I'll sneak back to bed.

But she stops and all I hear is her soft breathing. I shift my
body so that I can see more of the room from my hiding place,

and there she kneels, in much the same attitude as I had a few moments before, in front of the trunk.

Of course. From the moment Daddy slung it into the car, I'd thought of that trunk as mine. I'd wanted that treasure for so long, I'd forgotten that those objects had belonged to *her* mother, a woman she barely knew. Those bits of the past really belong to her, I guess. So, again, I wonder why it is now mine. Grace said in the letter that her granddaughter would "be waiting." I wasn't Grace's only grandchild, not even her only granddaughter, but Eva and Mary Nell had placed their sister's past into my hands without hesitation.

I can't see what Mother is doing, but I hear the crackle of paper and, thinking of that fragile bundle I had held in my hands, I jump from behind the sofa, click on the flashlight and yelp, "Wait! You'll tear it!"

"My God!" she says, putting up a hand to ward off the burst of light. "You scared me, girl!" She sits there with the trunk open and a half-drowsy, half-frightened expression on her face. I watch while it all dissolves into embarrassment.

"I was just on my way for a drink," she says, closing the lid. "And I . . . I don't know . . . I . . . um . . . got curious, I guess."

"I guess," I say. "Yeah."

"I mean, I know she left it to you, but . . . I've wondered for so long."

"Yeah, OK. Me too. I was looking before you came in."

She licks her lips and nods. I wonder why she looks scared.

"I haven't found much in there yet, but it looks interesting," I say, feeling around for the table lamp, turning it on and flicking off the flashlight. "I was afraid of waking you, but Daddy . . . well you know how deep he sleeps."

Mother already has the lid open again and holds the sheaf of papers. She looks at me inquiringly.

"A diary, I think. Somebody named Joy," I say.

My mother's eyes light up. "Joy! My grandmother. These must be really old." She works at the string and finally releases the knot. She closes the trunk lid again and spreads the paper on top.

" 'Mama don't move around much these days. She sits and pieces quilts,' " Mother reads. " 'Christmas . . . fine. Frank ate a lot and Sam was here with his wife and young uns and Mama make a big fuss over them but after they went home on down the road she sat for a long time lookin after them out the window.' " Mother stops and stares. We crouch side by side in that little pool of light coming from the lamp. "Frank . . . that's Granddaddy. I remember him, he was an Indian. He did seem to be eating all the time or thinking about eating all the time, but he never got fat."

I laugh. "Do we have pictures of him?"

"I've got one somewhere. It's not a good one, though. This must be Grandmama's. Joy's journal. I didn't know it existed. Wow." She looks at me and I find her obvious excitement fascinating. She isn't sing-out-loud excited, that wouldn't be her. But she brims with something that is part joy and part fear. I've never seen her look that way, not the completely composed Mrs. Dr. DuBose. I open my mouth to say—I'm not sure what—but she's already rebundling the papers and slipping them back inside the trunk.

"We've got church in the morning, Lizzie," she says. "We can spend all afternoon looking through this stuff, OK? You'd better go back to bed."

She puts her hand on the lid, but hesitates.

"Don't you want to see it?" I ask then, softly.

"What?" She frowns, her eyes still scanning the contents of the trunk. I can't even begin to guess why she pretends that it means little to her. She isn't good at it.

"Grandmama's letter. She mentions you in it."

Her body stiffens, so much so that I could see the knot of flesh form between her shoulder blades through her whisper of a nightgown.

"And . . . what did she have to say about me? Couldn't have been much . . . I was so small when she last saw me . . ." Mother thumps her palm against the leather lid as she closes it.

"Wait . . . I'll show you. Maybe you'll understand it."

I run to my bedroom to get the letter and run back, stopping for a moment in the living room doorway to watch her, still kneeling there, stroking the trunk idly, while her mind seems to be away somewhere else. Or sometime else.

"She just wanted you to be safe," I say, coming into the room again.

"Safe from what? From having a mother?" A tiny bitterness uglies her voice. But her expression remains bland.

"I don't know, Mother. Here." I hand the yellowing letter to her and watch her read, watch her lips move over the words *I could not curse her with these things.*

"Crazy. Yes, that would explain some things." Mother sighs, folding the paper and starting to unfold her legs. "Although I think most of Johnson Creek had already figured that out about her."

"But what did she mean, 'Maybe Sarah will be safe?' What was she keeping you safe from? And why would she give me

these things? How did she even know she'd have a granddaughter?"

"Why wouldn't she have one? Surely she'd expect at least
one of her children to have a daughter."

"But Aunt Eva gave it to me. Why did she give it to me? I'm
not Grace's only granddaughter." The questions fall out of my
mouth in a steady stream that I can't seem to stop.

"I don't know," my mother said wearily, getting to her feet.
"Maybe because you're the most convenient. I just know she
didn't leave it to me." She picks up the flashlight and takes it
back into the kitchen. She comes out and turns out the living
room light, her hand pressed into the small of my back, pushing me back to bed.

"You're asking me to get into the mind of a crazy country
woman who died more than twenty years ago," she says. She
bows her head and I see her pass a hand over her eyes. Is she
crying? She won't lift her head. "I'm the last person you should
be asking. The answer to all of your questions is I don't know.
I'll probably never know. All the answers are in the grave with
her."

She opens my palm and puts the letter in it.

"Go to bed," she says.

I stand in the doorway of my bedroom watching her pad
down the hall, sure that this is not the end of it. No, it's just the
beginning.

It gets even more interesting the next day.

Mother spreads Grace's quilt on the living room floor and sits
at its edge, like a small animal beached on the shore of a great
ocean. She wears white pumps and her peach-colored silk dress

with the white collar, and still holds in one hand the funeral-home fan that she inadvertently took from church. Daddy, leaning his six-foot-four-inches against the doorway to the dining room, dabs at a coffee stain on his white shirt and then considers the quilt from behind his steaming cup.

I balance myself on the arm of the sofa, clutching Grace's letter and watching the shapes and colors dance. Daddy had insisted that we take everything out of the trunk and this was what was underneath the papers and stuff. Now-faded pictures skim its surface, people run lightly across, time moves and there is, everywhere, water.

It is obviously the quilt Grace referred to in her letter, the one that she hoped would help her solve her problem, whatever that had been.

Mother's eyes have glazed over a bit. Trance-like, she touches an appliqué of a child. "I used to have a dress that color," she murmurs.

Daddy comes into the living room and squats down to look. "So, what was the big secret?" he asks, casually sipping. I hope he doesn't spill coffee on it. "It's all really interesting. But no reason to hide it away, is there? All that mystery, all that talk about giving it at the right time to the right person." He rolls his eyes. "That trunk should be your property, shouldn't it, Sarah?"

"The letter says quite clearly that Mama wanted it to go to a granddaughter. I guess Eva thought Lizzie should be the granddaughter and that now was the time," says Mother, breathing deep and fanning herself. She still stares at the quilt. "What kind of quilt is that anyway? Just some pictures stuck to a background. No rhyme or reason. She wrote about it like it was supposed to mean something." She looks over at me, sitting on the sofa.

Of course the pictures mean something. I follow two figures walking down a road with baskets on their heads. A woman and a child. Their footprints stride behind side-by-side and then the smaller prints—the child's—branch off and end at the edge of a large body of water.

It's a story. My skin tingles just below the surface. My arms ache and I massage one and then the other, gently.

"Looks like it ended up with the right person, though," says Mother. "Just mysterious enough and quirky enough for Lizzie, don't you think, John?" She smiles at me, but there is no light in her eyes. I feel as if I'm hurting her and I don't know what to do to make it stop. Mother can just have the whole thing, if she wants. But she doesn't seem to. Despite her obvious curiosity, she keeps referring to it as "Lizzie's trunk. Lizzie's quilt."

I hold her eyes for a moment, but she looks away and stares at the living room wall. I follow her eyes and meet the long-ago gaze of Grace Mobley Lancaster, who seems to take in the whole room from that flat, faded photograph that hangs there among other dead family members. *What were you thinking?* I ask her silently.

Daddy begins folding the quilt and Mother gets up with a little shake of her head and begins helping him.

"Yeah," says Daddy. "This all fits you, Lizzie. Strange letters, quilts and old dusty bits of the past. I think your Grandma Grace must have had some kind of premonition about you."

"Why don't you take it, Mother?" I say, watching my mother's downturned face. "It really is yours, don't you think?"

"No, it's not mine." She puts the quilt back in the bottom of the trunk and begins piling things on top. Daddy disappears into the kitchen for what I know will be cup number two.

"Besides," she says, shrugging. "My mother's been gone for a long time. What good is some old quilt to me?" Something lingers on the other side of her words. Sadness, maybe. Something that tugs at my heart and won't let go.

On nights like this, dreams come soft.

I lie half-fading into sleep, and a brown woman marches across the bed, wading through the moonlight. She is wrapped in color, a woman-child beside her. She adds her footprints to others on the road to the market, on the threads laid on the surface of my bed.

The quilt engulfs the twin bed, and I have folded it in half. I am safe underneath the story of my life; the brown woman is safe underneath my palm. On her way to the market.

It is hot, but I pull the quilt up to my chin. As always when the moon is full, I have drawn the curtain back to drink in the night. The room is bright as day, but the twilight world of dreams has arrived.

My mother has her hand on my head. I know it is my mother, though her face is unfamiliar.

"We have a long way. We must start," she says in a strange language. It isn't the weary voice of Mrs. Dr. Sarah Lancaster DuBose speaking her college-bred English; music falls from the lips of a full-brown woman. She gives me a small basket to carry, her eyes smiling, her mouth stern.

"Take this," she says. I don't know why I understand, and I don't stop to look in the basket; I know it's full of cloth. I balance it on my head and she hoists her own basket. We are going to market together.

The road stretches in an empty line. A rock stings me, and I pause to see the dirt gathered around my bare toes and wonder. Mother never lets me go barefoot. But as the thought flashes, my mother is a dozen steps ahead; her somewhat narrow body moves her loose wrapper this and that way as she walks. And when I run to catch her, she smiles at me inquiringly, but it isn't Mrs. Dr. DuBose; it is the full-brown woman, her head caressed by bright cloth. I smile back. I love going to market, because my mother is a master dyer. My father sings songs about her, his first wife, his only wife, by the fire at night while I drink in the night.

When I wake to bright Alabama day, there is dust about my feet.

June 1994 — Tuskegee

My father gives me his 1965 red Mustang convertible. Surprises me, but I take it. I might be two steps from crazy, but I'm no dummy. I understand that he has rewarded me for being on the right side of normal. More where that came from, his weary eyes promise as he hands me the keys. If I stay right. Everybody in Tuskegee knows that car. Cherry red, white leather interior, original chrome hubcaps. No one drives it except my father; he won't let Mother near it. It is the only object in his life that is the least bit—uninhibited.

I go out and about in it my second day back—slowly, I haven't driven a car in years; hell, I don't even have a driver's license anymore—and everyone honks. I put the top down to invite the June sun in and let my sweat stain the seats. Necks flex as the occupants of passing vehicles realize it is not Dr. DuBose driving, but a stranger—a woman with practically no hair who sings loudly through the town on her way to the grocery store.

I suppose if I had kept the hair—those shoulder-length ringlets that I used to toss as often as possible—folks would have at least had a chance to recognize me. Tuskegee is the kind of town where people don't change much. Women walk into Lou's House of Beauty every other Saturday and put on the same heads of hair they've worn for decades. Or they sit at home in their kitchens where bootleg beauticians wield hot combs or plastic gloves and tubs of relaxer. Men sit in the sun outside of Mr. Clark's tiny barber shop, waiting their turn. They get their trims and shaves, and frown at the Tuskegee University students who roar through town with dreadlocks flying.

Yeah, the hair might have been a giveaway, but the curls by Revlon are gone, as are the three-inch, petal-pink fingernails and tweezed brows. No teenager here, just a thirty-four-year-old woman who spent her first day back home yesterday staring at her blue-and-white bedroom, with the stuffed bears on the bed, the Prince poster on the wall, the teeny-bopper clothes in the closet.

It was all the same, mostly, as the day I'd left fourteen years ago. That day they'd loaded me into an ambulance, bandaged about the wrists, for a ride to a hospital room with bars on the windows. Now, all these years later, I have the eerie feeling I'm living life in reverse. I guess I am just expected to pick up where I left off at age fourteen, from before that trunk came into our lives.

But very old eyes had looked back at me from the mirror over the fake white French provincial dresser. The burnt-honey skin pulls so tight around my bones these days, making me look slightly surprised all the time, and my large eyes, like the hungry eyes of some animal, are all over my face. I'm all pared down, the surplus whittled away by bland hospital food and energy-sapping mental ramblings.

It's not too bad of a look, though. My hands fit nicely around my head, now that the hair hugs the scalp.

Moving one hand off the steering wheel, I run my palms over the crinkly springiness of born-again kinks. Mother had complained for years about that short, nappy hair. But, her hairdresser, Lou, doesn't make house calls at Bentwood Mental Health Center in Montgomery—or Smith-Rainey Residential Treatment Center in Birmingham or Parkside Hospital in Atlanta. And after the first few weeks at Bentwood, in a room with little in it but sheets and a nightgown, those chemical curls on my head began to grow heavy. One day I got an attendant to cut them, and I slipped into my real hair, feeling clean.

Now Mother perhaps will want to throw some lye on it right away, but I'll find some way to distract her.

Hell, I think as I shift gears and pull into the grocery store parking lot, *Prince doesn't even use his real name anymore. Things change.*

When I get back home with the cheese and eggs for the macaroni and cheese Mother plans to make that night, she is in my room, her head buried in my closet.

We'd begun cleaning it out that morning, and Mother had dived in with a relish that was unabated, even after several hours of filling boxes and flinging dust.

"No, no," I say, coming in as she is about to toss still another '70s relic into a cardboard box positioned near the doorway of my bedroom. "Don't put that in."

Mother looks at the blue cotton shirt she holds in her hand and then back at me. "Why not?" she asks.

"I need it for something." I take it from her limp fingers, fold it and add it to a stack on my bed. She shrugs and dives back into the closet.

"What are you going to do with those old things? I said I'd buy you some new clothes, Lizzie." She pulls out a pair of black patent leather shoes and laughs before tossing them into the box.

"A project," I answer. "Why didn't you and Daddy get rid of this stuff?"

"Well . . . it's yours." She throws something else in; I peep into the box, but decide to leave it. "After that . . . time . . . " Her voice trails into a jerky sigh. "I didn't know what to do . . . I just knew you'd be back in a week or so."

"Funny how time flies," I say, trying really hard to keep the sarcasm out of my voice but not hard enough because I see her wince. I guess I'm still a little mad. I'm not supposed to be mad. I'm supposed to be reclaiming my family.

I glance at her profile, noting the pucker just above her eyebrows. "Sorry," I say.

"Well," she says briskly, closing the box lid and anchoring it with masking tape. "It's done with. Behind us. You got through it all and you're all right now, right?"

My mouth opens, then closes. *Am* I all right, down inside this lie? I can't say, and she is gone anyway, looking for another box.

Riding around in the convertible is probably the first thing I did back home. Cleaning out the closet, the second. Talk about a time warp.

And the third? Grace's trunk. I look for the trunk.

When I ask Mother about it, she always finds a way to get busy. Really busy.

"Now," she will say, as she rearranges the corner of a rug that keeps slipping underfoot in the foyer, "I'm trying to recall where—I kept it in the attic . . . but no, I had to move it for that other box. You know, baby, I'm not sure where that trunk is right now. But it'll turn up."

Now, Mother never misplaces anything. She knows when the centerpiece of papier-mâché fruit cradled in the crystal bowl on the dining room table is one centimeter off-kilter. There used to be a woman who came in once a week to "do" for Mother and she got her feelings hurt a lot until she understood her place and our place and the way things were supposed to be. Our house is a shrine to middle-class order. Not just neat, not just clean, but true to the standards demanded by our position in this little belch of a town. Mother has a place for everything, including herself, and I know the whereabouts of that trunk are a mystery only to me.

I spend two whole days looking for it. The attic first, then all the closets and crannies about the house. I remember the attic being a sweatbox in summer, but now there is a big fan going on the roof, creating a slight breeze through the top of the house.

When I can't find it, I ask her again, and Mrs. Dr. DuBose looks so scared that I shut up. I mean, she is a sixty-year-old woman completely unaware of her own immortality. She might have a heart attack if she thinks I'm losing it—again.

The logic is good. Out of sight, out of mind; or in my case, not out of my mind. Not that I ever was. But she doesn't know that.

That last decade in the crazy house, I had fantasized about buying food, about the mundane act of pushing a grocery cart and selecting my taste's desire from the shelves. So although Mother and Daddy are surprised by my frequent offers to do the grocery shopping, I see it as the fulfillment of a years-old dream. They decide the Winn-Dixie is a kind of safe haven, so every other day or so, I end up there.

The only trouble with the Winn-Dixie is that you see everybody you ever knew in there if you go often enough. My second time in there I rounded a corner to find my old fifth-grade teacher staring, not at my face in recognition, but at my scarred wrists.

She aims her buggy in my direction and I think, *I'm just trying to buy some oranges. I'm just trying to buy some oranges and this woman is going to try me.*

Her name pops up from somewhere. Mrs. Penn. *Why does everyone seem to shrink?* I wonder, as she cautiously approaches. I know I've turned into an Amazon since grade school, but surely she is smaller. How does there get to be less of you? How does the body just fold up like that? I very quickly make a request to God. Being nearly six feet, I don't think my body would take very well to folding.

Mrs. Penn is well turned out in a crisp white dress—looks like linen—and a small white hat firmly atop coal-black, shiny hair. I think it is the hair I recognize and not the face. Her buggy in front for protection, she slip-slides toward me in white terry bedroom mules—totally out of place with the rest of her. "Well," murmurs Mrs. Penn, parking alongside me with painstaking care. A loaf of white bread and a tomato lie in the bottom of her buggy. "Well. Elizabeth DuBose. Uh-huh. I thought it was you. How are you, girl?"

I try to recall something about her besides the name and the rather useless fact that I once sat in a wooden desk in her class-room—middle aisle, three rows back—at Our Lady of Mercy. I remember being disappointed that she wasn't a nun. I'd always been taught by nuns until then, and they fascinated me with their pink faces and their pink hands that disappeared beneath their voluminous clothes, only reappearing to point or hit. Our Lady—the church and the parish school—is an island of luke-warm Catholicism in a town that teems with black Baptists and Methodists. Mrs. Penn was the first black teacher I had, and I guess that is how I placed her at all; a miracle, really, consider-ing all the many years of mental disorder between us—and I'm not just thinking of my vacation from accepted society.

Looking at her softly triumphant expression, I know she con-siders herself quite brave today, seeing as how she is looking straight into the eyes of a pure-tee, board-certified crazy person.

"Mrs. Penn," I say, leaning a little closer, hoping to scare her. "You're looking well."

She stands her ground, even inching closer. I'm mildly sur-prised, even a little proud of her.

"I try, baby. I see you're back." Her lips stretch into a smile I recognize from a couple of decades ago. "They treat you all right in there?"

She whispers now, then releases her death grip on the buggy and pats my hand.

"I don't know yet, Mrs. Penn, whether they treated me all right or not. When I find out I'll let you know." I really don't know. I'm alive. My thoughts now march to the right rhythm. So maybe they did treat me all right.

"All right, then, baby." She withdraws her hand. "So, what are you up to now?"

"Um." Can't answer that one. "I . . . I really just got here. Helping Mother around the house and stuff . . . you know."

"Well." She laughs, and I hear sarcasm. Or am I too sensitive? "It's not like you have to work, right? Your daddy . . . well, you can take your time. Did you ever finish at Tuskegee University? You were such a good student. High school val, weren't you?"

"Yes, ma'am. And no, I didn't finish college."

"Um-hum. I thought so. I remember you being real good in school, though."

Escape. Just around the corner of that aisle. I just begin to consider sliding the buggy that way when Mrs. Penn says, "Well, I've got to finish here. You tell your daddy I asked about him, hmmm?"

She takes the helm of her buggy once more and moves off.

March 22, 1899

Frank got Mama garden turned over. She say she gon wait another week though cause she say more frost comin. Meantime she makin a little dress. Feed sack dress embroidered with flowers for the girl baby she say is comin. Aint no baby comin Mama I say. I been married a long time now and aint no baby come. You know how me and Frank pray for one. But she act like she dont hear. She cant get here cause Im in the way she say. But when Im gone she come to take my place. She gon know thangs the one thats comin. She'll know things and that knowin be a gift from me her family thats lost. And I say Mama I get tired of you talkin all bout stuff that aint real. And she say you can get tired all you want Joy Im gonna tell it till I die.

"**Y**ou can't spread with those cards from the middle, Ruth. That's not the rules."

"But that's what I need!"

"You shoulda picked it up last time. Put those back."

My cousin Ruth throws down the four cards she has picked up from the stack and they slither across Grace's old quilt. We use my bed as a card table for gin rummy, each of us balanced on two hips with legs folded tailor-style. Cards hit the surface of the cloth, adding their colors to the parade of sewn pictures. Six-ounce Cokes make rings on the fake French provincial bedside table.

"Next pull from the deck and you're dead," I say.

"Un-un."

"You still talking to Danny?"

"We're talking." Ruth looks confusedly at the dozen or so cards in her hand; she rearranges a couple of them. "You and Lyman still talking?" She laughs. "What am I saying? You are."

"Ly-man," I say, smiling. "My baby. Gin."

"Oh, fuck."

"Don't let Mother hear you!"

"Sarah's in the kitchen." Ruth gathers up the cards and begins shuffling for the next hand, then stops. "You and Lyman . . . you done it yet?"

"It?" I know what she means.

"You got down with him?"

"Ain't none of your business."

"Don't let Sarah hear you say ain't," Ruth says teasingly.

"She's in the kitchen."

My mother's pots and pans clang, and she sings something unintelligible. Cards fly across the bed. Ruth deals out five each.

"What you wanna know about Lyman and me for?" I ask.

"I wondered, that's all."

I look at her, with her little-girl face and wisps of hair flying out from that braided bun, her most sophisticated hairstyle. She is Aunt Mary Nell's son's daughter, a year younger than me, the closest thing to a sister I have.

"Danny's putting the pressure on, huh?" I peep from around the cards fanned out in my hand. "Don't be too quick to do it!"

"Why not?" Ruth screws up her face in a who-the-hell-are-you-to-talk pout. "You did it."

"That's none of your business."

"I know you and Lyman did it, so you can't tell me nothin'."

"But we ain't talking about Lyman, we talking about Danny.

Not the same thing. And I'm seventeen." I pull a card from the deck.

"You can't tell me what to do."

"Sure I can," I say smiling. But I know I can't. And I can't tell her why I worry about her and Danny, because I don't know why. Lyman I can handle. Matter of fact, our first time was depressingly uninspiring. Had to be more to it than that. I tried to tell him, but he was deeply immersed in some male bliss I didn't get at all. And things never got much better. But Danny. Every time I think about him and Ruth I'm chilled.

"You could do a whole lot better than Danny, that's all," I tell her. "Why waste yourself on that dude?"

Now I've made her really defensive.

"But he's having such a hard time at home and everything, Lizzie. I gotta be there for him, don't I? Ain't that what I'm supposed to do? Every time he talks about his dad and everything I feel so sad for him."

"He's playing you, girl." I throw down a spread—ace, king, queen. "No girl of mine needs that kind of mess going on in her love life."

"Girl of mine?" Ruth laughs. "Oh, shit. You're starting to sound like Mama."

"Oh, don't say shit, that's so nasty for a young lady. You don't have to say that word."

"Huh?" Ruth puts down her cards and looks at me. When I look back, her face seems farther away than it did a moment before. "What's your problem? You say it all the time, Lizzie."

"Well . . . well . . . I shouldn't be doing that." I put my cards down too, spreading my fingers on the quilt. Beneath my hand, my foremother Ayo marches by her mama's side.

My eyes fall on the trunk, on the floor at the foot of the bed. When I first opened it three years ago and read the diary and the stories Ayo told to her daughter Joy, I had felt an incredible yearning to be in that room with them, to look into Ayo's face and see . . . I don't know. To see Africa. I wanted to be Joy, sitting next to my mother, pencil in hand, and I wanted to be Ayo, sitting next to my child, my future.

"He told me his father won't be home this weekend," says Ruth, her voice seeming to come from a distance, but breaking my train of thought nevertheless. "I think I'm ready."

Ready? A little ball of fear forms in the pit of my stomach as I look at her. The girl across from me returns my gaze, perplexed, as if she doesn't quite know me. "You stay away from that boy," I say. "I know I haven't always been here for you, but you have to believe I know what I'm talking about."

The girl just stares, her jaw slightly dropped.

"You know," I say faintly, "you look just like her."

"Who?" The girl's expression is so strange. "Who, Lizzie?"

I don't feel at all grounded. It is as if I'm floating a little above the scene, and I put my hand on top of my head, trying to hold it on my shoulders.

"Lizzie? Girl, what is wrong with you?"

Anger, warm and immediate, surges through my veins. "Is that any way to talk to me? What kinda tone is that, Joy? You really fresh talking to your mother that way."

"Oh, my Lord." She gets off the bed, backing towards the door. "Sarah!" The girl bangs the door open, bumping into the frame before disappearing. I hear her screaming through the house. "Sarah! Something's wrong with Lizzie! Quick!"

When the two of them come into the room, I am on the floor.

Don't remember how I got there, groveling on that blue carpet. I'm tangled in the quilt, but it feels good to be in that cloth womb, because I am cold. I wonder what day it is. Saturday?

The woman bends over me, her face contorted in fear. The calm voice that comes out of that face is itself a frightening thing. I can't remember her name.

"Sarah, I don't know what it is, but she called me somebody else's name and then I swear it was like somebody else was sitting there across from me." The girl rubs her shaking hands up and down the front of her jeans. "She called me Joy. Joy . . . ? Joy Ward?"

"It's all right, Ruth," the woman says, quietly, evenly, though her brown eyes are wild with terror. "Go call the doctor at the hospital. The number's on the kitchen board. Tell him Lizzie's sick."

I hear the girl stomp out of the room again, but I can't see her.

"Joy?" I ask. The room has dimmed. The edges of objects in the room have receded, only the woman's face, framed in the middle of my vision, remains and she is quickly fading. "It's getting dark."

"Oh, God."

I am aware that the woman sits on the floor with me, and my head is in her lap, but I can't see her anymore. I only feel her bones beneath my bones, holding me up. I strain to see, even though I feel the sun on my skin, coming through that window.

The light comes back in patches, and I stand in the sun. I have on work pants and a shirt. I am in Johnson Creek.

The Baptist church I joined as a child, which I remember as regal, but worn, grows out of the ground in front of me clothed in dazzling white. I recognize the site, but stand there in silent amazement. A ragged voice calls "Lizzie, Lizzie!" but it merely echoes. The sound of hammering and the voices of sweating men fill all the spaces between the pines. I look down at my hands, at fingers I barely remember. They are dark and rough and ache slightly around the joints. But they are mine.

I walk towards the church and look through the windows, not the ones I'm used to, the ones covered with the dust of the ages. I see through the clear glass to the other side of the building, where a girl of fifteen or so is talking to a tall young man with straight black hair. He plucks the blade of a saw and laughs at the twanging sound it makes. I feel a headache coming on, and walk around the building.

She has her back to me, and he sees me first. He glances down at the ground sheepishly, and she turns, looking exasperated when she sees who it is.

"Hey, Miz Bessie," the man says. He is an Indian, ruddy-brown-skinned and long limbed. "Uh, I gotta get moving." With swift steps, he moves off, swinging the saw, climbs the steps and disappears into the church. I freeze, staring after him, 'cause I know I've been in this scene before. Going to the window, I see him with five or six other men who are working on something at the end of the church. After a moment, I realize they are building a pulpit, and a snapshot appears in my head: the worn wood of the church pulpit I know and the threadbare altar cloth that hangs there.

"Mama, I was just talking," the girl says from just over my shoulder. "Frank and me was just talking. We wasn't doing nothing."

"You stay away from that boy, Joy!" I whip my head around, surprised at the rush of anger that comes to me at the mention of his name. I know that name. Creek Indian boy from down by the little river. There is a picture in my mind of the house he and his mother and brothers live in.

I realize as I look again into the church that I know the name of every man in there. And I know the name of the girl standing in front of me, too.

Joy. My daughter. She pouts, fingering her carefully braided hair. I notice the skirt she wears is long. Only the tips of her brown boots stick out.

"Ain't you supposed to be learnin' ?" I ask. "Why ain't you over at Miz Tilly's?"

"She let us go. We through today."

"Then you shoulda gone home 'stead of over here. You don't need to be over here."

"Mama . . ."

I shake my head at her.

"You and that indun gonna be the death of me," I say, smiling a little bit at her pretty pouting. Her face—the sculpted cheekbones, full lips and wide eyes shining—become more familiar by the moment. "You got plenty of time for that," I say, jerking my head towards the building, and Frank Mobley. "You better put something in yo' head 'sides him."

"You know I am, Mama," Joy says. "But ain't but so far I can go with Miz Tilly. I know how to read and write. Add up things a little. Don' know what else is there."

"I don't know either." I look across the road that runs in front of the church, looking for Son Jackson's house. There is a tiny cabin there, brand new. I know I am here, but it's like a dream.

"We gon' just see how far we can go, you hear? But readin' . . . well, I like that readin' you do. That's a great thing."

"Mama, you know me and Frank . . ."

"I don' wanna hear about Frank Mobley. I don' wanna hear. He too old for you anyway. I need to go talk to his mama 'bout him hanging round."

"But he eighteen, Mama. That not too old."

"Go home, now. There's work to do there. Go on." I watch her move away. She's so graceful, so sure of herself. Frank looks out the window, but ducks back inside when he sees me staring back at him.

I go and sit on the church steps. It smells like May. The scent of this place never changes. I watch a swirl of red dust—a dust devil—spin towards me along the road, and close my eyes in anticipation of dirt flying.

I open them back in my blue-and-white bedroom in Tuskegee. The memory of long-ago Johnson Creek still moves across my consciousness like a cloud on the horizon. Something approaching, but just out of eyesight. I hear a soft rumble, as if thunder's coming.

My father sits by my bed trying to feed me. I don't know how long it has been since I fell on the floor and Ruth ran away yelling. I focus on his face, which looks decidedly grim. He balances a plate on his lap.

"I wish you could tell me what's happening to you, Elizabeth," Daddy says. "You know it's been a whole day and you haven't said a word, except to mumble in your sleep. And I can't find a thing wrong with you."

Can't talk now, Daddy. I'm watching the horizon.

"Ruth was just here. You scared her to death yesterday."

I saw Joy, Daddy. I saw my daughter.

I close my eyes. It must have been, what? After the war. Freedom had come and gone. The church was gleaming white. And I heard the sound of men talking mixed with the hammering and they, Joy and Frank and everybody, were all ground to dust by the weight of the years between that moment in the sun and this . . . this suddenly hellish afternoon.

"Joy," I whisper.

"Joy?" Daddy shakes me gently by the shoulder. "Elizabeth? Ruth said you called her by that name. You must be mixed-up, honey. Your middle name is Joyce, not Joy."

My lids open slowly; I shake my head, but I can't make my mouth form any words. I am tired. My eyes slide lazily around in the sockets like lead weights.

Daddy puts two tablets in my hand. I swallow them silently, then rub my fingers over my wrists; the skin feels raw. He retires to a chair, looking lost, and Mother comes into the room.

"Sarah, who is Joy?" my father asks. "Do we know a Joy?"

"Oh," she said. "Only Joy I know of was my grandmother; she's the one who wrote the diary, the book we found in the trunk. But Lizzie didn't know her."

"Yessss. . . . That's right. That can't be who she's talking about, though."

Joy, I said silently, I saw Joy.

July 1994—Johnson Creek

When I call my great-aunt Eva, she tells me the trunk and the quilt are back at her house. It doesn't take me long to get going. My mother, anxious about my driving down to Johnson Creek by myself, goes with me, balled up in the passenger seat of the red Mustang.

I hum right along without a driver's license. The only one I ever had expired long ago, while I was silently busy in Nuthouse No. 1. Mother doesn't seem to remember this and I don't remind her.

Mother can't drive a stick anyway, and even if she could she wouldn't dare drive the Mustang.

So here we go. Every bend in the road seems ancient. As I turn onto the dirt-and-gravel track that leads to Eva's house and Son Jackson's and the church, I think about old summers spent running, sweating in the sun. Old and young. Old and young at the same time. No wonder I always felt misplaced.

Aunt Eva has her garden hat on. Coming around the curve to her house, I see those large plastic flowers around the wide brim, the ones that stopped being yellow a long time ago.

Eighty-six years don't look like nothing on her. Most days, she looks younger than her daughter, Patricia, who sometimes stays with her. But then Aunt Eva was only fifteen when she had her.

"I got some ice tea made," she says from the front steps, as Mother and I get out of the car.

"Where's Pat?" Mother asks. "Is she here today?"

"She went to Union Springs to the bank for me." Eva takes off the hat, smooths her hair, which is pulled into a soft, white knot, and goes inside.

"That trunk is in Mary Nell's room, Lizzie," she says, disappearing into the kitchen.

Mother stiffens. I suspect she let our reason for coming slip away until that moment. She gives me what can only be called a fearful look and follows her aunt. "Why'd you even have to tell her where it was, Aunt Eva?" I hear Mother whisper urgently. "That damn thing."

"And you think she's forgotten it all?" Eva answers. I lose their voices as I make my way back to Mary Nell's room.

It is immaculate and seemingly unchanged since her funeral. I pick up the familiar photograph—Grace, Mary Nell, Eva, in that sassy pose—and smile. Remember the day, tucked away back in my soul somewhere. I try to put the photo back exactly in the same place and then I sit on Mary Nell's bed. I miss her. I feel as if she lingers close by, a smiling spirit. It's a little like that moment in March when you step out onto the porch and smell spring—just a whiff of something invisible and silent, something that is just coming or just gone.

The familiar leather trunk squats casually across the room in front of Mary Nell's thinking chair.

I kneel before it, as I have in times past, smiling at the trademark creak of its hinges as I ease it open. The scent that escapes from under the lid is the same. Ancient. The quilt rests on top this time, angrily crumpled. My mother packed the trunk, I suppose. I unfold it slowly, spread it out on the wood-plank floor and try to smooth the wrinkles, an almost impossible task after so many years of its being jammed in a ball and crushed.

The cloth is even more faded than I remember, and here and there mottled with now-brown bloodstains.

My mother, my poor Sarah. I try to picture the moment—fourteen years ago, I guess—that she had thrust the quilt back into its Pandora's box. Had she been crying that night she and Daddy returned from Bentwood to a silent house and my bloody room? Yes, I think, as I stretch my long body out on top of the cloth, laying my cheek on the creased picture of the full-brown woman and closing my eyes. Sarah had cried. And she had looked at this thing and cursed her own mother and put it as far away from her as possible.

I sit up and stick my hand inside the trunk. I find the sheaf of papers that is Joy's journal and gingerly place it in my lap. A certain rush of happy relief surprises me; I am free, I remember. These things can't hurt me anymore. The story on those diary pages belongs to me, but they don't own me. My memories live somewhere spacious now; the airless chamber of horrors has melted into the ground. I guess psychotherapy, psychiatry and long-term residential treatment really cured me of something. Cured me of fear. Made me live with every part of myself every day. Cured me of the certainty that I was lost.

I open the packet of papers and choose a sheet at random.

"Mama always talked strange when she tole them ole stories," Joy writes. "She never los that strange voice of hers from Afraca, but when she talked about her childhood and the bad times it seem like she really was Ayo and not Bessie after all. She once told me that Ayo got los when she crossed the water. Bessie kinda took over."

And Bessie became Grace, and Grace became me. Me, Lizzie.

I put the papers down and reach into the trunk for a small leather bag. Opening it and pushing aside two stones, I draw out something blue. The scrap of indigo-dyed cotton feels like a cloud in my palm, insubstantial and hardly graspable.

That bit of nothingness is the only thing I have left of the master dyer. She had colored that cloth for me. A bigger piece makes up the dress of the girl child appliquéd onto the quilt, on her way to market, basket on her head. They tore the cloth from my body that day by the sea facing west, but I held on, held on to something, balled it in my fist forever. Now, I look at what's left, wishing that I remembered the name of the full-brown woman.

"I made it, Mama," I whisper, putting the cloth away in the leather bag and picking up the tattered grass doll that lies beside it. "I'm alive. Can you hear me?"

The doll is Joy's. I made it for her so, so long ago. It is hardly recognizable as a doll, but it still smells like Johnson Creek when Johnson Creek was younger. Like the cloth, it is falling apart, becoming dust as I watch, and here I am, older than the lives I spread before me, with the blood surging through my veins like spring rain.

I lay back down on the quilt, holding the doll to my chest, happy to be alive but missing everyone. I don't even realize I've closed my eyes until I hear Mother's voice approaching.

"That girl's still got problems," I hear her say as she moves towards me, trying to whisper, but forgetting that the long tunnel of a hall amplifies everything.

"She ain't no girl, Sarah. Been a woman for quite some time." Aunt Eva's voice comes very clear in contrast to my mother's anxious, shaky tones. Mother's words always sound trembly, perched just above some frightening unknown with the ledge crumbling beneath her feet.

I think things get even more shaky for her when she enters Mary Nell's room and sees me there, stretched full-length on the quilt, clutching the disintegrating doll. Her audible intake of breath speaks volumes.

"What are you doing? Why can't you just leave that thing alone?" Mother snaps, gesturing toward the quilt.

"Because it's mine," I say quietly. "I'm going to take it back home with me. The whole trunk, as a matter of fact."

"Why? Look, Lizzie, it's not worth it. It's not worth . . ." She stops and stands there, wrapping her arms around her body and biting her lip. Eva comes up and slips an arm around Mother's shoulders.

"I'm OK, Mother," I say, placing the doll back in the trunk and standing up. I begin folding the quilt. "See," I say. "I'm touching it and nothing's happening."

"Not funny, Lizzie," Mother says.

"I'm not trying to be. I just want you to know that there's

nothing happening here. No craziness happening here, Mother. I . . ."

"Lizzie," Eva says softly, giving me a warning look that silences any other comment from me. "I saved you a glass of tea in the kitchen. Don't bother with that trunk now. I can get Mr. Jackson to put it in the car when you're ready to leave."

Mother again inhales sharply, wrenches herself away from Eva's embrace and hurries out of the room.

"Take it slow," Eva says to me, smiling slightly. "Someday she'll understand better."

"I don't know, Eva," I answer, lowering the folded cloth back into the trunk and closing the lid. When I look up from my task she is at the dresser, fingering the framed photograph.

"Yes she will, baby," she says. "You can be a gentle person. But when something needs doing, you don't let it go. Never have. That's why you're here now. Because you left something unfinished. But I know you. You won't feel right until you take care of it."

"I not sure I know how."

Eva shrugs and takes my arm, moving toward the hallway. "Find a way," she says. "Find a way."

April 12, 1899

Its a real good day. Mama and I sat out under the pear tree behind the house. There are still some white flowers on it and everythin smells good. Mama say I wont be here to see another. Another what Mama I say. Spring she say. Dont say so, Mama. Dont say so. Its all right she say and she got this smile on her face. Im sure I find somewheres to go I always do. I was always a wanderer. That's somethin else I wanted to tell you daughter cause it was my wanderin in a way that landed me here right here on this spot talkin to you. I know she bout to tell one of her stories that she so crazy to have me rite down. So I run into the house and get the paper and pencil and she wait under the tree. Mama always talk strange when she tole them ole stories. She never los that strange voice of hers from Afraca, but when she talk about her child-hood and the bad times it seem like she really was Ayo and not Bessie after all. She once told me that Ayo got los when she crossed the water. Bessie kinda took over. She had to think like her not like Ayo from Afraca. I didnt understand that at first.

When I came back she was starin off. I came here on miserys back she said. You remember daughter how fast life can change. It was a simple thang. Gon to the market. Watchin people. Listnin to my Mama voice as she call out to the folk passin. Singin bout cloth she had. It was so simple a thang to be there in the smells and the smoke and the rumble of peoples voices both close by and far away over the hills and between the houses. I was at that age where my curiosity was a growin livin thang that was hungry inside a me and moved my feet along places where my mother tole young feet not to go.

But on one day when I was just 14 seasons from the day of my birth I was wit her in the market. She sat her beautiful dyed cloth spread round. I sat too but I had only been a minute when that restless I talked about kinda seized me made my eyes wander away from my mothers side. And soon my feet was followin my eyes roamin the distant dusty alleys lookin lookin lookin. And down one way I went and felt someone lookin back. I los my family that day I los my home that day. Daughter I have always been a wanderer. My mind went places and my feet followed. My mother worried all the time. Joy you learn to watch the trails in the dust left by the feet of yo children. You read they minds. The very thang that brings them joy may lead to they greatest pain and yours. So my mother learned. Because my wanderin brought me over through livin death and started new roads in a new land.

February 1980 — Tuskegee

The TV blares *Days of Our Lives*. The Oreo cookies I indulged in as soon as I came home from class have done nothing to focus my mind on studying art history.

It is hard to take the Impressionists seriously while wrapped in Ayo's glorious quilt. Maybe if we sample a little Romare Bearden, I can relate.

My bed is too inviting, so I have moved to the living room, dragging the quilt behind me. But no amount of fidgeting can keep me awake.

A quick nap. A brief rest before jumping into the books again. I turn over on the sofa, pulling the quilt close under my chin. Mother will fuss if she catches me here, rumpling the velvet throw pillows. But I'll be gone before she returns.

Nothing wrong with a little dream, I think as I gather the fabric in one hand and draw it over my shoulders.

I am sleepy, but I can't seem to doze off. I stare at the wall for a few moments, at the fading photographs of old souls. There are mostly women in those photos, mostly looking grim or lost, but one person in particular, my grandmother Grace, gazes back with the most faraway expression. Dressed in a light-colored blouse and long dark skirt, she sits beside what looks like a dressing table, cheek in palm. She gazes somewhere past the photographer's shoulder, into another land. And though she sits serenely, she still seems poised to move, to get up and immediately go somewhere, anywhere, away from there.

I feel a silly, sympathetic smile tease my lips as I look at her. The longer I look, the closer she comes, closer every time I blink my heavy lids.

Sighing, I close my eyes and turn over on the sofa. I sink in, watching colored lights dance on the inside of my eyelids. Sometimes the colors turn into pictures, skipping back and forth too quickly to be read. In flashes, I still see her looking—Grace—I wonder what the problem was.

A sound startles me. Something clattering, falling. My eyes fly open and I look down. At my feet a hairbrush lay on the wood floor, and as I bend to pick it up I absently consider the fact that my mother's new carpet, the carpet just installed three months ago, seems to have disappeared.

When I straighten, I catch a glimpse of myself in a mirror. The face that looks back is both familiar and strange, strange enough to make me drop the hairbrush again. Then I realize that I'm sitting, not lying down. I'm at the dressing table. In a chair. And it is Grace's face that looks back at me from the glass, her flesh-and-blood, three-dimensional face, looking very surprised inside its frame of very black hair. I half expect to look out a window and see myself stretched on Sarah DuBose's good sofa.

There *is* a window, but what I see are pink roses climbing about the sill and, beyond, a barbwire fence, a pasture, cows lumbering up and down little hills.

I turn again to the mirror and watch as Grace begins to tremble.

"Mama!" A whirlwind of flying hair and small legs bursts into the room, a bedroom, I now notice, a bedroom with a wood-plank floor. The child carries a round basket that is almost bigger than she is.

"Sarah, baby, slow down!" I hear the words come out of my mouth, and I gasp. Even as I say it, the child, a girl of four or five, stumbles and trips, launching the basket and a kaleidoscope of cloth, thread and buttons. In a split second, the floor is covered with various sewing objects and Sarah—for that's who it is, I know without hesitation—is beside the dressing table, out of breath and trying desperately not to spill her tears as well. Buttons and pins make tinkling sounds, like hard and soft rain, as they roll across the floor.

"Brought your basket, Mama . . ." she says, biting her little lip and rolling slowly until she sits leaning against my leg. "Owww . . . my hand hurt . . ."

For a moment I can't think, can't feel my body in this place. I can only see the scene before me, see little Sarah's head, full of small, neat plaits, lost in the folds of the skirt Grace wears. Then an eerily familiar sensation brushes across my skin, the soft opening and closing of a door between adjacent worlds. I have been moving in and out of mental landscapes with increasing frequency in the past two years, waking dreams constructed of strange vague memories. Often I find scratches and small raw scars on my body.

I remember I've had this dream once before, a few weeks ago, watching Grace and a little girl do something in this room together. But I had watched, not participated. And now I reach down and brush Sarah's hair with shaking fingers. And now I know Grace and I are together here. I just can't remember what to do next.

Sarah tries a small smile, even though her eyes are drowning. "I sorry," she says. She goes over to the bed, stopping to right the upended basket, and struggles to pick up something and drag it over to me. "Can I help you sew, Mama? You said you'd show me."

"Baby, don't drag it in all that dust and junk. And be careful; there are pins all over the floor," I hear myself saying. Or is it Grace saying it? I don't know. I'm so well-cocooned inside her past that words flow from me automatically.

I hold out my hands and Sarah puts a piece of cloth in them.

It is the quilt. Grace's quilt. At least it will be. I run my fingers over the still-bright colors and notice the places on the background waiting to be filled.

"What's the matter, Mama?" the child asks, placing her hand on my knee.

"What's the matter with you, girl? Why don't you go into the bedroom and sleep?"

Sarah—Mother, full-grown and frowning—stands over me holding the quilt, which she begins folding. I roll over on my back, feeling the muscles stiffen and ache. My shirt irritates my skin.

"I know you're tired, Lizzie, but you can take a nap in your own bed, can't you? It's hard enough trying to keep things straight around here without you lounging on everything."

I stare at her, trying to find the child's face behind her down-turned expression, fighting to get my bearings. My whole body hurts.

"Sarah," I say. "You remember that quilt of mine?"

"Don't call me Sarah. That's so common. I'm your mother. What quilt? This one?" She shakes it at me.

"You remember when you helped me sew some of the pieces. You wanted me to teach you how to quilt. You were . . . five maybe. Do you remember that?"

"Lizzie, what are you talking about? Get up off that sofa and go sleep in your own bed." She hands me the quilt.

She isn't listening. She is already thinking about what Daddy wants for dinner and about the finger foods for her eight o'clock sorority meeting. She doesn't hear me.

I get up slowly, painfully. The whole episode didn't feel like a dream, but I must have slept, and in an awkward position.

"Come here," I say, grabbing her hand and leading her to my room. I spread the quilt on the bed. "You remember this quilt? Remember when . . . it was being sewn?" I'm almost startled by how faded the quilt looks now.

"Well, no . . . I told you when we first saw this quilt. I remember my mother sewed a lot. That's about the only memory I have of her, really. She kept her things in a . . . she had a . . ." Her arms make a circle.

"A basket? Big and round, with her threads and things in it?"

"Yes." She frowns at me, but I see she is still preoccupied. "I didn't know I'd told you that. Look, baby, I gotta go start dinner and make those sandwiches and things. Go on and take your nap, but stay out of the living room, OK?"

I watch her bustle away, always in a hurry, but never smiling like the young Sarah of my dreams.

That night, Grace returns.

I'm in my room in search of sleep; I stare at the wall and Prince's black-lined eyes stare back from a poster. That feels spooky, so I close my lids.

When I open them again, Grace is with me—or I am with her. Her husband, George, is here with both of us, there in our house in Johnson Creek. He lies quietly in bed, sleeping, but slumber is now the farthest thing from my mind. Grace wraps her thoughts around my mind and I sit there with her in the grip of a quiet fear that makes it hard to breathe.

If she sleeps, she fears the return of the dreams that follow. The scenes of water and blood and death.

The moon rises so fast, Grace sees it moving across the sky and wants to jump the pasture fence and catch a ride. But she can't because her dreams will follow.

She'll put a moon in the quilt. She'll put her smiling Sarah and her funny, funny twin boys in the quilt. And her beautiful man, George, who laughs with his eyes. So she can remember them. So that Grandmother Ayo doesn't drown them with the past. She'll put them on the edge, small-like.

I sit on the old bed with Grace, marveling that I can move her fingers and toes. Slowly her pain finds every part of me. We hurt, our body hurts. Arms and ankles and back. Everything is heavy.

Ayo—Bessie—has invaded Grace's memories and she can't keep things straight in her head. Ayo is there, reminding us who we are. And we can't stop the sea from rolling beneath us and we can't stop the fear. The chains go on over our skin, no matter how much we holler. We don't understand what the white ones say and they don't understand us, but they know they are hurting us, don't they?

Softly, Grace leaves the bed and finds the quilt, folded over the back of a chair. She sits with it on the floor, wondering what to do.

Her fingers trail the edges of an appliquéd figure, and she touches the cloth that she's sewn around the body of the full-brown woman. The one who walks with her hips only and her feet gliding above the dust.

A sob makes its way to the back of her throat. *I've lost my head,* she thinks, *and George will have to put me away.*

Mary Nell and Eva have told her that the thing to do is keep it all inside, hidden and quiet. But she can't. It comes out. She talks in her sleep and George asks about it the next day. Things come out when she just talks, talks about normal things. And some days, her body hurts so much she wants to die, but there is no reason for the pain. If she stays, George will put her away someplace, locked up, and her sisters and her mother won't be able to stop him.

The light from the moon falls on his face. The part of me that is Lizzie is afraid to touch him, while Grace just sits there already missing him.

Something on the floor glints in the glow coming through the window. Pins from where Sarah spilled them earlier that day and Grace failed to find them. As she leans over and grabs them, she sees that she's missed some cloth scraps too, there under the bed. She spreads them out on the floor and one piece in particular draws her eye. Blue. A closer look in the moonlight tells her it is that beautiful blue piece that her mother, Joy, had given her. It came from Grandmama, from Ayo. Joy had always kept it. There isn't enough of it to do nothing with, she said, though Grace had known her mother to do much more with much less.

Grace pins it to the quilt, just to the right of the swaying woman.

There will be a moon on the quilt. And pictures of George and her sons, Frank and Phillip. Mama, Joy. And Sarah, smiling baby Sarah. So she won't forget.

August 1995 — Tuskegee

Mother's face clouds when I show her the bag of cloth.

"That's what you wanted with all those old clothes from your closet? Some of them were good enough to give to the Goodwill.

"What kind of quilt are you thinking of making?" she asks, digging her hand into the bag and running her fingers through the fabric. We're in my bedroom and I have pulled two brown paper sacks from the bottom of my closet.

"Appliqué," I say. "Like Grandmama Grace's."

She takes a deep breath. "Well . . . I don't know how to do appliqué. Do you?"

"Oh, yeah. Somebody showed me."

"When did you get so interested in quilting anyway?"

"Well, Grace's was so beautiful. I've thought about it for years, doing something like it. And fabric would be a new artistic medium for me. I've dabbled in just about everything else."

Her eyes widen. "You have?"

"Sure." I close the bag and shove it back in the closet. "Rehab, you know. Occupational therapy. Keep the mind and hands busy and maybe they won't wander."

"Don't. Don't joke about it." She doesn't look at me, but at the floor.

"OK. I'm sorry, Mother."

"I don't know why," she bursts out, "you want to do this quilt thing, when it was that . . . that . . . that started all of this!"

Her fear becomes a swirling current in the room. But I have to continue the story, and maybe, please God, Mother will understand in the process. Her fingers brush mine and she takes my hand, applying an amazing amount of pressure for someone with such small fingers.

"I couldn't stand it if . . . if something happened and you had to go back to the hospital," she says, her eyes watering. "You know that, don't you? You know why this quilt is a bad idea?"

"I'm over all that, Mother," I say, my arm going around her shoulders. "No more of that. It's over with. I just need something to do until I get my shit together. You know, Aunt Mary Nell's and Aunt Eva's quilts were always so beautiful."

She sighs and I feel her muscles relax a little. But though her face, as always, stays calm, her eyes search mine for a place to hide from her fear. She is silent, and I add, "It's a project, not a relapse."

Red, I think, for Grace.

But spring pastels jam the window of Mrs. Quincy's fabric store—little-girl pinks, sky blues and pale, buttery yellows. No good. The edge of my new quilt needs blood red. Blood binds three lives, and I already have a jumble of fabric scraps at home, waiting.

"Mrs. Quincy, do you have any red? Just a nice clear red."

"I don't know, baby." The woman in the bright orange slacks turns around and around among the mountains of material. How can she not know? She's owned the fabric shop since the beginning of creation and some of this cloth has to have been here since then. "I'll go back here and look."

Over at the remnant table I search for anything that looks usable, listening to Mrs. Quincy's mutterings from the back room. The little bell on the front door rings, but I don't turn around.

"I'll be right out," she shouts.

"No problem," a well-water deep voice calls back.

Celibacy, voluntary or not, really weakens you. Don't let anybody on any spiritual quest convince you otherwise. If your sexual urges don't ruin your search for enlightenment, they will ruin something else. So after a few minutes, I admit to myself that I am weak, that maybe there is more than one way to truth, and peek not so subtly over my shoulder.

I recognize him, but the name doesn't come to me. That's no surprise. Every black person in town—and there are a lot of black people in this town—went to the same high school, the same scout troops, the same parades, the same funerals. And everybody is somebody's somebody: somebody's cousin, husband, brother, sister, lover.

His eyebrows arch and a question forms on his lower lip, which moves in the most tantalizing manner. In a few seconds his inevitable query will pop out and I try to get a quick look at everything beforehand—tight chest in a denim shirt, dimpled chin graced with a whisper of dark beard, long-lashed brown eyes set in a face that is deep-dyed in chocolate satin.

He points a large hand at me, snapping his fingers.

"Hey," he says, smiling. "Don't leave me hangin' here. I know we know each other."

"I'm not leaving you," I say. God, no. "I'm hanging too."

"OK, OK. Class of '80?"

Damn, I thought, younger. Well, only a little. Younger could be good.

"No," I say, " '78."

He laughs. "Help me out."

"Elizabeth DuBose. Lizzie."

"Yeah, that sounds familiar. Anthony Paul." He sticks out his hand and I lose mine in it.

"Two first names," I say, like an idiot.

"Yeah." He stares. He smiles. Dimples deepen.

Mrs. Quincy barrels out of her mysterious back rooms with two bolts of red cloth.

"Sorry," she says, dropping them on a table and invoking a small dust storm. "This is all I have." She turns to Anthony Paul. "What do you need, young man?"

"Just curtain rings," he answers, following her to a far corner.

Unrolling the top bolt of red, I remember that he didn't start, or even blink, when I said my name. So maybe not everyone in town knows my illustrious history. My self-absorption (or is it paranoia?) amuses me. Maybe folks actually had better things to think about than me during the past fifteen years.

The first red is too orangy and it has some small pattern on it. Little circles or something. The second looks better, but the flimsy fabric feels like it's been lying in the dust since the turn of the century. In a year or two, it will be dust as well. I'm telling Grace's story with this quilt—just as she had told Ayo's story with hers—and the fabric has to hold up at least until the next storyteller comes along.

I restack the bolts and consider a trip the next day to Montgomery or Auburn.

"You kin to Dr. John DuBose?" Anthony Paul stands behind me, clutching a handful of curtain rings.

"My father," I say cautiously.

"Yeah, not that many DuBoses in town. He's in my fraternity chapter."

"Alpha Phi Alpha forever, huh?"

"Well." He grins a little. "I don't know about that. But it does give men an excuse to act full of themselves every once in a while. We seem to need that."

This statement impresses me and I hope my raised eyebrows tell him so.

"Nice seeing you, Mr. Paul." I shoulder my bag and hold out my hand.

"Yes. Nice. Miss DuBose." He grasps my fingers firmly and quickly leaves them tingling.

"Thanks, Miz Quincy," I call, as I make for the door. "But I guess I'll keep looking."

The street outside swims in the heat. The wind keeps things tolerable. A man I don't recognize waves to me from across the square. I just nod back. It has been a year and I guess people are getting used to seeing me around. I imagine their conversations about me: "If she crazy, she sho' don't show it."

But Anthony Paul doesn't seem to be aware of any of that. I venture a glance over my shoulder and see him through the shop window, bending his tall body to hear something Mrs. Quincy is saying.

A car pulls up beside me. A couple of people had stopped earlier today to offer rides, but I wasn't interested, so I decide to ignore this one. Then I hear an annoyed voice say, "Elizabeth, get in."

Daddy runs a hand over his graying hair, looking exasperated, almost angry, as I climb into his navy BMW. "Why didn't you drive? If I'd known I would have given you a ride downtown," he says.

"I wanted to walk. Feels good to come and go without asking anybody's permission."

"Oh, I get it." His sarcasm thickens the air between us. "Listen, I'm not trying to be your jailer; I just wish you'd . . ."

"Do what you want? Make you feel comfortable about me being home, right? You're not comfortable with it, Daddy, so I might as well do what I want. I'm thirty-four years old, almost thirty-five. I'm OK. I'm not going to try and hurt myself, so you can leave me alone once in a while."

"I just want you to be safe."

"I'm as safe as the next person. You make me feel like I'm twelve, and I'm a lot older than that. Frankly, I'm bored as hell. Being sane has got to be the dullest thing in the world. How do you stand it?" I don't know why I feel like hurting him.

He grunts, but says nothing to that as he turns down Main.

"I'm going to go down to Montgomery tomorrow, just so you know," I say.

"Good."

"Maybe I'll stay overnight. I'm thinking about looking for a job. Dr. Ramsey has been after me to start thinking about working or something." I'm glad it pops out of my mouth sounding so casual.

"No," Daddy says flatly. "He should know better than that. That's not the right thing for you to do."

"Didn't we just go over this thing about, you know, my being thirty-four and mentally safe and everything?"

"Come on, Lizzie! A job? You've never been able to hold down a job. Remember? Remember that last job you had in college? Half the time customers would come up to you and you'd look through them like they weren't even there."

"Well the head docs have gone and taken the little voices away, Daddy. And I've got to do something. What's the point of going through all that if I'm going to just sit and watch Mother dust and make pink-and-green tea sandwiches? I'm so glad I'm home, really, but I guess I envisioned something more. Maybe not a job, but . . . I don't know. For the past year I've done nothing except gain ten pounds." I wish I didn't sound so brattish. "I gotta do something sometime."

"Go back to school."

"Oh, OK. I'm not together enough to hold down some brainless job, but I am together enough to plunge back into academia. Daddy . . . I washed out, you know?"

"Think about it. You can't get anything good without college anyway."

As I stare out of the window at the white lines on the asphalt shooting straight and sure down the highway, that creepy feeling begins to sneak up on me again, that feeling of looking back into time at some distant point and feeling more familiar with that place than with where I am now.

That sensation is still with me later that day when I show

Mother some of the sketches I've done for the new quilt. The figure that dominates the pictures so far is of a tall woman with a trunk.

"So this woman," Mother says, picking up a sketch from where I've laid it on the dining room table. In it, Grace is packing. "She's going somewhere?"

"She's a traveling woman," I say, looking over her shoulder at the image. A tune rambles through my head.

" 'I'm a traveling woman, I got a traveling mind, I'm gonna buy me a ticket, and ease on down the line . . .' " I sing softly.

"What is that?" asks Mother. "It sounds familiar."

"Just an old song I picked up somewhere." I lay out the fabric pieces, while she fingers my sketches one by one.

"She's holding the moon," Mother says, running a pink-tipped finger over the paper.

"She's sitting in the moonlight," I say, "and the moon looks so big she thinks she'd like to reach out and take it with her, because she's not so sure it shines so brilliantly where she's going."

My mother turns her whole body around to stare up at me, rolling her eyes. "Where is that from—some book or something?"

"I don't remember, Mother. I guess somebody at the hospital told me."

"OK. OK," she murmurs softly, letting the paper fall back to the table. "Is that what you thought about while you were in there, quilts and trunks?"

"Among other things. I thought about my past a lot."

"I really hoped you would change your mind and do a

pieced quilt," she says. "I don't know anything about appliqué. Are you sure you want me to help you with it?"

"Oh, yes. I'm not going to do it without you. And it's not hard," I say, "Grandmama used to do it."

"What did you say?"

"Grandmama used to make appliqué quilts sometimes. The quilt she left me was appliquéd."

"I know, but for a minute . . ." She sighs. "You spoke as if you were there, watching her make them. You always *did* sound so sure about it, so sure about your so-called past when all the time you were . . ." She stops and lowers her eyes.

"Crazy? You can say that if you want, Mother. Of course, just because I know you think I'm crazy doesn't mean *I* think I'm crazy."

"Huh?" She looks so puzzled that I laugh, and she smiles a little.

I sit in a chair and begin rummaging through the basket where I've collected some sewing tools.

"Do you have little scissors, Mother? These big things won't work."

"Lizzie," she says as she digs down into her own sewing bag, "I don't understand. Did somebody show you this appliqué stuff in the hospital?"

Yeah, I think. Like they'd give us scissors, needles and seam rippers. That would be like saying, "We give up; go ahead and gouge your eyes out, slash yourself, chop off the hair of your fellow crazy person while they nap in the day room (actually this did happen to a woman at Bentwood while I was there; the intrepid barber was quite exuberant, and was never punished. The instrument of destruction was never found).

"I took a class while I was at that place in Birmingham," I lie. "Anything to subdue the masses."

Sarah hands me a pair of small scissors and watches as I cut a tiny dress for Grace from an old flowered shirt I used to wear to summer Girl Scout camp. A traveling dress. There is brown silk from one of Daddy's ties for Grace herself.

"Was it bad?" she asks.

"Huh? Great, these cut better."

"Was it bad?"

"What?"

"Those places."

I can't answer for a moment. I don't know the answer. I realize that I don't know if I am sane or not. It's all a matter of point of view anyway.

"They were fine . . . I mean, they were hospitals, Mother, and I wasn't in to get my tonsils out," I say as cheerfully as possible. "It was just lonely sometimes. But I'm here now."

She flashes a brief, half-hearted smile and sits down next to me, fingering a cloth cutout of Grace's trunk.

"Why don't you sew that on for me?" I say, taking it from her and pinning it to the background fabric. I show her a few stitches and then hand her the needle.

"I wish Mama had taught me more about sewing," she says. "All I do is replace buttons."

"You never talk about her, Mother," I say, looking over and sighing at the huge stitches she is making. "No, sweetie, that stitching is supposed to be invisible. You gotta make them that small."

"Not much to talk about," she says. "I came back from my

Grandmother Joy's one day and she was gone. Aunt Eva and
Mary Nell—they taught me some about quilting. But they always said Grace was better than the two of them put together."

I keep my head bent over the cloth I'm supposed to be cutting, almost paralyzed by the pain that stabs my chest. I take a
deep breath before starting to snip again.

"This woman here." Sarah picks up something I've just cut
out. "She looks like she knows where she's going. Determined
to get there."

"How can you tell?"

"She's got a long stride to her. Moving with purpose."

"But," I say, "she's looking back. She wasn't sure where she
was going, only sure that she had to go."

"Hmmm." She considers it for a minute. "In a hurry, but
scared."

"Yes, exactly."

"Scared of what? You gonna show me the rest of the story?"
She looks me square in the eye.

"It's coming."

Mother puts down her sewing and picks up the drawings
piled in the middle of the dining room table. She shuffles them,
like cards. Those scenes have come to me from deep-buried,
but ever-present memory. Treasures from the vault.

I remember standing on the steps with Eva and Mary Nell in
our Easter dresses. Wandering through the house in the middle
of the night trying to find sleep, because the pictures wouldn't
stop. Catching the train north. Working on the assembly line.

"You're such a good artist, baby," Mother says, holding up a
sketch, and I wondered how she could hold her own mother's

story in her hands and not recognize it. Maybe she'll never be able to open the door to the possibility that I could have been right about being Grace. About being Ayo.

I watch her trace the outline of Grace's figure.

"You know," she says, "no matter how much you try there's no way you can know about Grace's life."

"You know this quilt is about Grace." It's a statement from me, not a question.

"Yes, Lizzie." She sighs. "And I'll help you with it. But after this, no more fantasizing about her. Your obsession with this is just as scary now as it was then. She left. She died. That's it."

My doctors talked a lot about denial. Every time I calmly explained to them that I knew reincarnation was real because Grace and I were living it, they said very pointedly, "You're in denial, Elizabeth."

My mother wore her denial all over her face; she could stand there and stack the sketches that told her all she ever yearned to know and hide behind the well-worn idea that I was once again becoming delusional.

She could pretend that her mother was merely an unpleasant memory, someone she could die mourning, though I was right here waiting to embrace her as my child.

When Grace lived in Detroit and worked in the war factory, she had a one-room apartment where she entertained her lovers. She liked laughing, sweet-voiced men with country Southern tones that floated out in the air and kissed her cheek. They made one recall the taste of sugar cane even while deep in the womb of a Northern winter, and they all had some story of home that made Grace think of Johnson Creek.

In some cavern of my mind, I remember their voices.

Grace had a record player on which she would play stripped-down blues songs. She had a tea set with delicate china cups from which she served gin and tonics. She had three cloth dolls, all with the same little brown faces, that she had made herself.

And she had her quilt. From the moment she had arrived, she had slept under it, unfinished though it was. At first she had just laid the pieces on top of the bedcovers and after many nights of sitting bent over in the second-hand rocking chair sewing, it became large enough to warm her sorrow, though not to excise it.

I spend the rest of the day lost in that image of Grace, and that night after helping Mother with the dinner dishes, I'm in my room with my sketch pad, trying to put a picture to it all to go into the new quilt too.

I draw a picture of Grace in bed, lying under a tiny replica of her quilt, then close my sketch pad and turn off the light.

Immediately, the moonlight bursts in through the window and I pull the quilt, Grace's mourning cloth, over my heart.

April 24, 1899

Mama be moanin in her sleep. She say its only old memory comin to visit. Last night she be in the next room moanin like that and cryin and Frank wake up and say whats wrong with her. I went in and Mama just layin there in the moon beams kickin the covers. I just watch her Im afraid to get her up. Then she sit up in bed sudden and stare at me with sweat comin down her cheeks and forehead. For a while its like she dont no me then she grab my hand and yell rite this down! and I get up and run out to the other room. Frank had turned over and was snorin. When I got back to the room with the paper Mama is mumblin to herself. You rite fast Joy she say. I aint gon tell this but once. It too bad to tell more than once.

I think when the man grab me in the market I kick him but he put his hand over my mouth and nose and I cant get no air. So I fall out. Faint right away. And when I come back to myself Im lyin on some sand and there are others there. Strangers with iron round they arms and legs. I saw a child walkin and cryin so I get up on my knees to go to him but I cant cause my hands, my feet chained together with iron too! Oh child! I am chained to the man next to me and when I look at him, he look like he weepin. I dont know if its tears or sweat but his face is balled up and his mouth moving, saying words I dont know. I start to scream. I call my mamas name. I scream and scream. Over the sweatin shoulders of those chained together people the ocean rushes and rolls. I remember starin out at that water going on and on to the edge of the earth even while I screamed so hard my nose start to bleed. And this . . . this ghost with hair like fire and no color eyes comes over and hit me cross the head with his hand. Yes daughter that was the first white man I ever saw and though I done met some since who was gentler I never met none any less cruel.

February 1980 — Tuskegee

OK. I was sitting up in bed and then I wasn't here. I looked from the eyes of another person. A person now dead. I had a husband, I had children. I lived in a house where the moonlight touched the bed. I went out for a long moment and I was back. Wasn't I?

I don't know who to tell. Not them, the parents, who'll say I was dreaming. No, I was there. I was Grace. And Grace was having a problem. Her grandmother was bothering her. Grandmother Bessie, I remembered thinking—Ayo, with her past of blood and water.

Gotta be a dream. I was just sitting here, daydreaming a little, getting sleepy, and I fell asleep, I guess. Been doing a lot of that lately.

Aunt Mary Nell would have said that the ghosts were strolling.

"It's hot and dusty and crazy up there," Ruth says, watching me dig around in the bottom of my bedroom closet. "Atlanta ain't no place to be in summer."

"So you think that foundation of yours can spare you for one weekend?" I can't find my new linen sandals.

"Yeah. No fund-raising for a while. I guess we've picked the pocket of every snooty Atlantan by now anyway. And Mama's been after me for a visit. She's not happy that I wanted to spend a night here. But she would never suggest that I not see you. 'She needs you so much now,' she said."

"Well, damn, I've been home almost a year. She still worried about me? In a way, she's right, though. I do need some company. It's nice to have a kindred spirit around. Mother certainly is not on my wavelength. I think she's choosing not to be." I abandon the closet and lift the dust ruffle of the bed. "Shit." The sandals are, unfortunately, smudged with dirt. I brush my hand over them in a futile attempt to clean them. "Shit. Ruth, do you . . . ?"

"Yeah," she says, grinning. "Look in my suitcase. Brown leather mules. You really think Sarah's gonna look at some quilt you're making and finally believe that you're her long-lost, long-dead mother?" Ruth snorts. "Good luck. She doesn't wanna believe."

"Maybe the quilt wasn't a good idea," I say, tossing her bag on the bed. "I mean yesterday she's standing there with the sketches in her hands, raising her eyebrows and giving me sad looks."

"Sometimes you have to cut off the part of your memory that hurts. Maybe that's what she's doing, you know?"

"Yes, dammit, I do know. I'm going to make the quilt whether she catches on or not, so . . . well, we'll see." I dig the mules out of Ruth's suitcase.

"I can't believe you gonna do this party. I know you're all strong and together, this whole new woman now, Lizzie. But do you really want to catch up with folks about what you've been doing since high school?"

"First of all," I say, "this is not a big deal. Just a few people from our class. They have a little picnic every year. I saw it in the paper. So I'm not going to be plunging into a shark pit. Just wading into a little deep water."

"If you say so." Ruth sighs. "Too bad that guy you met isn't going to be there. What class was he in? Was it mine?"

"No, '80."

"Hmmm." She rubs her chin and smiles, leers almost. "Slightly younger man. But not a child. Smooth."

"Stop it." I laugh, feeling a little embarrassed. I put the back-less shoes on and tuck the white linen shirt into my shorts. "I spoke to the man once for two minutes in a dusty store."

"But there were vibes, that's what you told me."

"Well, who wouldn't give me vibes? I haven't gotten any since . . . hell . . . I can't even remember."

"I bet I'd remember him if I saw him," Ruth says.

"You'll probably never see him. I don't think I'll be socializing with him once he starts asking around about me. Who knows what Mrs. Quincy told him."

"Yet you want to go and shoot the breeze with a bunch of people who know all too well where you've been for, like, fourteen years . . ." She frowns.

"Don't worry. It's just a little test I'm giving myself. I can hang."

I'm late. Years late, when you really think about it. They have set up a grill in Bobby Pine's backyard. I remember him as a tall boy, all arms and legs. Basketball star. Still tall, of course, but that slender frame has been invaded by a potbelly, the kind of growth that always looks abnormal on a thin body.

Bobby's yard backs up to the lake. When I arrive a knot of fifteen or so people are on the deck, watching the host wrestle with a huge slab of ribs.

Bobby's wife comes up to me, swinging her hair. Stretching her arms out, she grasps my shoulders with both hands, greeting me and holding me off at the same time. She sighs heavily, smiles perfectly. "Lizzie. I can't believe it's you. I'm so glad Bobby invited you."

I cannot, for the life of me, remember her name. She and Bobby started going together during our last year of high school. But I couldn't recall anything else about the woman.

"Yeah," I say. "Lucky for me I saw that thing in the paper."

Her smile fades some, but she manages to keep going, drawing up beside me with her arm around my shoulders and guiding me over to the deck.

"Well, of course, Bobby had heard you were back in town, but he wasn't sure . . . wasn't sure you were interested . . ." Her voice fades a little. Then it takes on a false brightness. "But I'm glad you called! We're happy you could make it."

I groan inside.

An hour later, I am about to make my move. I imagine unfolding my long legs from the lounge chair that has become glued to my butt and moving gracefully towards my hosts to mouth my good-byes. Then I see myself tossing back the rest of my gin and tonic and gliding out to my little red convertible before roaring off.

But I don't move. I close my eyes and twirl the stem of the glass and sink beneath the funk rhythms coming from the speakers set out on the deck. No one has come near me in the past half hour. No one has asked me about my former problem. Disappointing group. Draining the glass and setting it on the little metal table next to my chair, I start to do that unfolding. A hand on my shoulder stops me, though, and I look up, way up, into the expressionless face that had smiled so sumptuously that day in Mrs. Quincy's stifling fabric store.

"Going?" Anthony Paul asks.

"You're not in my class!" I blurt. "Why are you here?"

His bland expression breaks up—I can really see it melt down—and he smiles, then laughs. The deck crawlers turn their heads.

"I know Bobby. And you know what the social scene is like in Skegee. When you hear about something stirring, you go, 'cause it's likely to be the only game in town." He sits down, uninvited, on the edge of my lounger. "Thought I'd see what was going on over here." He looks around and I follow his eyes. "Not a helluva lot."

"No, I was just thinking of leaving," I say. "Damn. Why didn't I stay home?"

"Oh, nice. Just when I come along, you gotta say something like that." He looks genuinely crushed.

"No! It's not you—"

Maybe it's been so long since a man paid any attention to me that the protective layer around my hormones has broken down. Yeah, there it goes. Just got ripped away when this person smiled at me, which he did with great gusto. I haven't had to use that kind of shielding for many turns of the earth, but now . . . I better remember how it works, 'cause Anthony Paul has a invitation of some sort written all over his face.

"Really, though. I don't blame you for getting gone."

"Yeah. Well." I finally untangle my legs and stand up. "I better say good-bye to the hosts."

"Maybe I should too. I'll go with you." Then he leans over and whispers, "Just imagine how their jaws would drop if we leave together, smiling wickedly."

"You sound as if you'd enjoy that much too much," I answered, trying not to laugh. His generous lips crinkle a little at the corners.

"Oh, yeah," he says. "Bobby's not bad. But that woman of his . . . whew! You'd think she was at the convention when white folks invented snooty."

Jaws do not drop, but eyes widen as we say our good-byes and Anthony Paul strolls me to my car, his hand lightly pressed—in the most casually intimate way—against the small of my back.

I look back at the deck; the small clump of people assembled there look pretty much the way they did back when they were clinging together in the halls of the high school. I wonder where the other eighty or so class members are and how come I hadn't just ignored that notice in the paper—like they did.

"Great car," Anthony Paul says as I lean against the door of the Mustang. "I've seen Dr. DuBose in it."

I think maybe this is a good time to test his knowledge.

"Yeah, it used to be my father's pride and joy," I say. "But when I left the hospital last year, he gave it to me. A reward, you might say."

"Well, damn, Liz," he says, his smile unchanged. "I was hoping we wouldn't cut to it quite so quick."

"It?"

"Your . . . illness. Is that what they call it these days? When I asked my dad about you, of course he told me. But I was hoping . . . well, hoping that you would reveal all to me in some pleasant, intimate setting, over some very nice dinner or something. You know?"

I know I'm staring at him, but I can't help that.

"Illness," I say gently. "That's a nice sympathetic word for it. Anyway, I thought that if you were going to transform from potential prince material into some kinda jackass, I'd rather find out sooner than later. And I'm not interested in being anybody's service project."

"Whew! You don't hold back, do ya?"

"I don't have time, Anthony Paul," I reply. "I've missed too much already."

August 16, 1899

Whats that like the sellin I ask Mama. Joy, I aint gon tell you that she says. I cant stand to tell you that.

September 1980—Johnson Creek

Ruth knows first.

We sit in the old apple tree behind Aunt Eva's house in Johnson Creek, having just delivered several basketfuls of apples to Aunt Eva. She watches us from the back porch where she peels some for canning.

My fantastic out-of-body story has my cousin sitting still as stone, her cheek against the rough bark of an upward-reaching branch. Funny, she doesn't look the least bit shocked, and she presses for details.

"Damn," she murmurs. "You did it again."

"Again?"

"Ah, I remember it well," she says, mockingly putting her hand to her chin and looking skyward. "Nineteen-seventy-seven, wasn't it? You called me by someone else's name, fell off the bed and stared in space for a couple of days. I wrote about it in my diary."

"But I never told you . . ."

"You never told me what you saw, Lizzie. But you called me Joy. Ancestor of ours, right? So's Grace. Why are these people trying to talk to you?"

"You make it sound like ordinary conversation."

"Well, I know it ain't that. But some kind of communication between then and now is going on here. I mean, is there funk after death?"

I roll my eyes.

"Was there something familiar about the house you were in, about the room?" she asks.

"Yeah, I told you. But I can't tell you where I'd seen it." I look off over the top of the house, the church, and towards the cemetery where Grace lay. "Maybe I was in Grace's house, you know, that old empty place back up in the woods where we used to play. But it wasn't anything like you'd remember, Ruth. It was . . . it was home, with furniture and rugs on the floor. It was like remembering, but more. I saw what she was seeing. I saw . . . man! I saw Mother as a little girl. When I woke up, or came to, or whatever, it didn't feel like a dream. Felt like I'd stepped out of one room and into another."

"You said you weren't asleep. Both times you winked out and then back?"

"But I had to be asleep, Ruth, right?" She is taking me far too seriously, frightening me.

"I don't know. Maybe Grace was trying to tell you something. And Bessie."

"Damn, girl. This ain't no *Twilight Zone* thing."

"No, much better." She grins. "The real stuff always is. So what else?"

"Well, I am kinda achy when I wink back in. Sore. Some places feel almost raw. But after a few hours I'm OK."

"Ooooh. Physical manifestations. Did you do something in the other times that hurt you? That could be proof that you really went."

"No." I look down at Aunt Eva, who has stopped peeling and now stares at us, not moving. She can't hear us, can she?

"Where are the pains?"

"My wrists and ankles and back. Stinging."

"Lemme see." She holds out her hands and I give her mine. Turning them over, she examines the wrists. "I don't see anything," she says, putting her fingers against my right arm. Then she is still. She puts her hands around my wrists and lets out a small gasp, dropping them as if they are hot.

"What? What?" I search her face, and her eyes are clouded.

"I felt something," she whispers.

"No shit. What?"

"Pain." Ruth closes her eyes. "Just for a second. Pain."

"What kind of pain? I don't feel anything, at least not now."

"But . . . oh Jesus, it's there! Just under your skin."

"Ruth." I touch her hand and she flinches. "What am I gonna do?"

"I don't know. But Lizzie . . ."

"Yes?"

"There's more coming. Coming fast." She keeps her eyes closed. Her lips tremble.

"Ruth . . . you can feel that?"

She nods.

"How?"

Ruth opens her eyes and says, "How is it that you can step into the life of a woman who died before you were born?"

"There is no answer to that," I say.

We stay at Aunt Eva's that weekend. We had driven down from Tuskegee in Ruth's new car after classes Friday to help with the apples and to taste the first pies, and had planned to go back that evening to catch a party on campus.

But after we climb down from the tree, we decide to stay. We call our mothers, who are playing cards with two other ladies at my house in Tuskegee. I imagine my father safely cocooned behind the door of his study, sipping and reading. Nothing can get me to go home and disturb such domesticity tonight.

"Can you touch me now?" I ask Ruth after dinner, after Aunt Eva is in bed and we sprawl on the front steps. She reaches out a hand and takes mine tensely, sliding her palms over the wrist and forearm. After a few seconds, I feel her relax.

"It's OK," she says, taking her hand back nevertheless.

We're sick, I think, as Ruth swats a lightning bug. *Very sick.*

That night I wake because the night chill has crept into my heart. I open my eyes and I'm standing upright under the night sky. My bare toes dig little depressions into the dirt road just beyond Aunt Eva's front porch, where I can sense, rather than see, Ruth standing, watching. Her long frame sways toward me.

Sleepwalking. That's a new twist. Can't remember the dream that brought me out here. Can't move until I remember what

I'm supposed to remember. It just feels so good to be out, but I can't move to what waits for me.

Closing my eyes, I try to remember. That pain is back, especially along the wrists. I rub them. I'm being pulled, but I can't go where they want me to go. Not there.

Ruth's eerie pitter-patter follows me, down the road a bit past Son Jackson's house, and then a turn right to the pasture that runs all the way down to the little river we call Johnson Creek. Our white nightgowns fly out from our legs, making us winged spirits, and Son Jackson's cows, standing still as stone a moment before, turn their long heads to look.

I stop and close my eyes. Salty air saps the moisture from my lips. Why am I here and why can't I go home, when I know my mother waits for me?

The ground slowly rolls under my feet. I smell—taste—sweat and blood and months of misery. The scent knocks me dizzy for a moment and I stumble forward. Then I am pulled, jerked. I open my eyes, but there is a void in front of me. Light, gray and weak, filters in slowly from the left side of my vision, and I see the deck, the water beyond and the line of dark bodies going jerkily forward into the ghost-land. Each bent back ahead of me is familiar.

A gurgling sob reaches me. Mine. I'd been steadily shuffling forward, but I can't go any farther.

The rail is under my palm, the weight of another person dangles from my wrist. The bottom of my foot scrapes the top of the rail; I try to ignore the sound of the chain dragging along the wooden deck. Trying to stand on the rail, I expect to be jerked back at any moment. I crouch there for what seems to be an eternity. The man attached to my wrist whispers to me urgently in some strange tongue. When I turn to look at him, there is some slow-crackling fire in his stare. I am to go, his eyes say, and he'll go with me.

So I throw my leg over the other side, but I feel myself being pulled. . . .

I hit the water with a hard thud, rolling over and scraping my forehead on something—is it the side of the boat? I touch bottom and the water is pitch-dark; no sunlight. Where is the sun?

A hand grabs me and my head breaks the surface. But I'm not sure I want to open my mouth to breathe.

"Dammit!" Ruth says, her voice coming from far away, but her fingers biting into my arm. "Help me—at least a little here, Lizzie! You're like a damn rock!" She drags me through the water crossways to the current; it tugs gently but insistently on my limbs.

I drift into that now-familiar sensation of disorientation; my mind crawls down a long hallway. I know Ruth is there, but when I look into her face, I see someone else. A dark girl in African clothes, silent but with eyes that speak of horrible things. She and I seem to walk back and forth, back and forth, holding on to each other.

Cold water slaps my face as I stumble and fall.

"Lizzie," I hear Ruth half-growl, half-moan. "Lizzie, don't blink out on me now!"

Hands in my armpits haul me upright again and I stand face-to-face with Ruth, chest-deep in the cold, tumbling flow of Johnson Creek. If Ruth looks that frightened, I wonder how I look. The African girl is gone. The ship deck is gone. Involuntarily, I touch my arms under the water, but I already know there are no chains.

"Lizzie . . ." Ruth strokes my forehead and then stares at the smear of blood and water on her fingers.

"Your head," she says. "You're bloody. Let's get the hell outta this water!"

We wade through to the shallows. Ruth scolds. I can think of no response to her mumbling, frightened questions.

The creek isn't very wide, but it's sort of deep in the middle. If I had dived over in the shallows, where the rocks ruled, that likely would have been the end of my story.

Over my shoulder, I see the thin-railed small-plank bridge that spans the stream. Luckily, I'd gone over in the deepest part with water to cushion the fall. Still—I touch a hand to my head as Ruth drags me by the arm to the bank—I hit something. Is that why I feel so fuzzy?

Despite the warmth of the night, we shiver violently as we stumble to shore, and we don't break stride until we are climbing Aunt Eva's porch steps.

Inside, Ruth almost tears the soaking nightgown off me, still whispering urgent questions at me as I stand there naked, hair dripping and on its way back to wherever hair goes, back to damn Africa, I guess. She searches for something dry. I can't answer her questions. I don't know what to say. Cursing, she wraps me in a sheet and slips away down the hall.

OK, OK, OK, I think, clutching the sheet closer. *Ayo-Bessie. Grace. Y'all just trying to confuse me.* Grace always speaks loudly, her memories hissing insistently inside my head. And behind her are the dream-like tangles of Ayo's life. More distant but also more painful. I shiver, wanting it all to go away immediately, but I still see the burning eyes of the man on the ship's deck, lit up with some fever.

"Lizzie," says Ruth, slipping back into the room and closing the door, "you got to say something to me so that I know you're doing all right here." She is still soaking wet. She drops a dry gown, one of Aunt Eva's, over my head.

"Lizzie?!" She grabs my arm, and we both gasp. A searing pain passes through my body, radiating from the wrist she has in her hand. Her eyes widen and she looks otherworldly, her body rigid with pain, her hair hanging limply against her chin, and the wet gown still glued to her body.

"Let go of me," I manage to choke out. "Please. It hurts."

But she hesitates, as if it is difficult to move. Finally she reaches up with her other hand and pries her own fingers from around my flesh. I slump, suddenly so tired, staring at the red, round marks on my wrists.

I watch her wearily take off the wet gown and put on another. She sits on the edge of the bed and begins drying her hair with a towel. She tosses me another dry towel and slips under the covers.

"Go to bed before you die shivering there, Lizzie," she says. "But don't touch me."

I turn off the light. Ruth breathes heavily beside me in the bed we share, and I try to scoot my body as close to the wall as possible.

"Don't tell the doctor," she says.

"What?" I turn my head to look at her, trying to see her face in the dark. I only discern the faint outlines of her cheek, her nose, her ear.

"I wouldn't tell your father or Sarah about what happened tonight if I were you," Ruth says.

"I wasn't going to."

"Good idea." Ruth turns her back towards me, and I sink down in the bed. I am afraid to sleep, since the line between dreaming and waking has become hard to see with the naked eye.

September 1995 — Montgomery

Dr. Ramsey has an annoying habit of continually clearing his throat. He tugs at his pants, which always seem to be falling down. He scratches his crotch when he thinks I'm not looking.

Now how am I to sit in the same room for an hour with that? Today I distract myself by reading the notes on his desk calendar upside down, while he strolls in front of his large window, looking out.

It's a good thing I don't really need psychiatric help, since this so-called doctor doesn't seem to know much about the hills and valleys of the human psyche. I am more qualified than he is.

"Everything seems to be going pretty smoothly with you, Liz," he says. "But I'm worried about your . . . drifting."

Upside down, I read MOTHER'S BIRTHDAY—PICK UP LONDON
FOG. I hate how he cuts off my name. Liz. Stupid white girl
name. I tell him it's Lizzie, and he decides what I tell him
doesn't matter.

"Explain what you mean by drifting," I say. "I thought I was
just living."

"You've been out . . . back more than a year, Liz. Don't you
want to get on with things? Work?"

"Maybe I'm not ready for that. My father doesn't think so."

"Do you think you're ready?"

I snort, reading upside down under Friday CALL JANET.

"You head doctors," I say. "Do you know how many times
I've heard that question? 'Do you think you're ready, Liz? What
do you think, Liz? Why do you do these things?' I can't believe
all of you spend aeons in school so that I can sit in your offices
and psychoanalyze myself!"

"Why are you angry at me? Besides, I'm not a psychoanalyst.
I'm a psychiatrist."

I get up from the chair. When will I be cured enough not to
go through this?

"I'm angry at you," I say, as quietly and slowly as I can, "because you ask me the most idiotic questions in the most serious
tone imaginable without giving me any answers that mean anything and because you take my father's money for this and because on a whim you can decide that this outburst warrants
another visit to the crazy house for me. That makes me angry,
doctor. And yes, I can still get angry without getting crazy, if
you know what I mean."

"I know what you mean. Sit down. I'm sorry if you're frustrated by these sessions, but I think you're doing well."

"You sounded as if you thought I was a deadbeat," I say. "I just haven't decided what's what yet, that's all."

He laughs and scratches his crotch.

"No, I don't think you're a deadbeat. It's just that you're an extremely smart woman who's not really making any plans for herself and I think you ought to."

"Yeah, OK. I'll start thinking more seriously about school, maybe. But right now, I'm just relearning life, OK?"

"OK." He sits behind his desk and scribbles. I drop into my seat again. He's crossed out the CALL JANET note on the calendar.

I laugh out loud and he looks up at me with those sad brown eyes set in that sagging face. *Does Janet even know he's breathing?* I wonder. He moves a wisp of hair that has fallen across his vision.

"I think you should give serious thought to what your next step will be," he says. "School is an option. Or maybe a part-time job. I can speak to your father if you like."

"I have thought about working," I admit. "But I can't quite put my finger on the right career move for me, Doc. I have a big time gap in my résumé."

"Maybe I can line something up."

"No." I stand to leave and hunt around the chair for my bag. "No, Doc. Let me handle this one."

He smiles, happy to let me handle it. He is too lazy to handle it. He would have made me some psychiatrist's receptionist and I would have pissed somebody off with my nonchalance and it all would have made life a little bit more uncomfortable for us all.

When I'd brought up the possibility of a job with Daddy, it was more to see his reaction than anything else. The truth is that

I'm not sure that I want to be distracted right now from what I had decided would be my main occupation—reclaiming my sixty-one-year-old daughter.

Still, I find myself telling her about the conversation with Dr. Ramsey.

We've taken the quilt project out of the dining room—Mother cannot abide the scraps of thread and fabric falling and becoming part of the carpet—and to the attic, where we sit under the crazy whirl of the fan. Its relentless spin moves the sunlight into rapidly moving patterns that dance against the roughly finished walls.

"You could tell better what was going on if the pictures were in a row," Mother grumbles, wiping the film of sweat from her forehead before continuing her task: tracing an outline from one of my drawings. "This is hopelessly jumbled."

Mother made it clear early in the quilt project that she finds the design unsettling. I look at the outline under her fingers, which draw tailor's chalk across midnight blue background fabric—the moments of a life moving in a semicircle: Grace pleads with the moon. Grace gathers her suitcases and wears her traveling hat on the trip north. The old porter pushes the trunk onto the train as she gazes out of the window for her last look at Alabama.

"Life," I say, "is nonlinear, Mother."

"Depends on how you look at it. You may see it as a circle. But it always seems like a line to me." She puts the chalk down and wipes her fingers daintily on a paper towel. "The past is past."

"Well, I like circles," I say nonchalantly. "The world seems to move in cycles, don't you think?"

She shrugs and gets up to stretch. There's no sound except for the turning fan blades—not unless you count the cacophony of thoughts careening around in my head. I want to stand up and declare myself to her, cry, "I am the circle! The circle stands before you!" But I don't. I begin telling her about the session instead.

She's soon smiling at my description of Ramsey's calendar entries.

"You should see him, Mother. It's so hard to picture him as a hot lover. But then maybe this Janet is just his speed. So anyway . . . I was watching him scratch himself . . ."

She giggles. A surprisingly young sound.

" . . . and the job thing comes up again. Now he's making me feel guilty about just lounging about in my parents' house, but I swear, I just don't have any occupation in mind at the moment."

Of course, Ruth is wanting me to join her in Atlanta at the foundation. She has her hands full running the homeless advocacy organization and calls down here every week or so asking for my help.

"What are you doing except sitting around anyway?" she would say.

"May I remind you, you selfish heifer, that I have something to take care of here?" I would answer.

"Hopeless," Ruth answered. "Face it. And I know people who really need your help. *I* really need your help."

"No," I always said before hanging up on Ruth's rather vocal disappointment. I couldn't leave yet. I had to finish the quilt.

I look now at my daughter/mother's head bowed over the table. She has taken up the chalk again in her long, slightly creased hand. Her diamonds, glittering from well-manicured fingers, love the sunlight.

This unfinished business with her and me—I feel as if I've come back from death and exile just for the moment when the light of recognition glows from her eyes. My stomach churns a little at the thought.

I hope she finds me in the quilt's story, but if she doesn't I'll try something else.

"Oh, damn." Sarah puts the tracing down in frustration. "My fingers are getting stiff."

"Take a break," I say.

"Yes, I think I will." She leans back and sips from the glass of lemonade she's left on the floor. "I think you should ask the twins about a job."

"The hardware store?"

"Sure. I mean, it doesn't have to be permanent. Just something to satisfy Dr. Ramsey that you're not idle. We can think of something else later."

"Well, not a bad idea, me among the hardware. But Uncle Phillip and Uncle Frank probably will consider me completely useless. I'm not mechanically inclined and they know it."

"Nonsense. You can just work the register or something."

"Daddy won't like it."

"What do you mean?"

"He wants me to go back to school. I have no idea what I would do there."

"There's plenty of time for that," says Sarah, lifting her head towards the window. "Did I hear a car?"

In the driveway below, Anthony Paul unfolds himself from a black utility. I stand with my forehead against the glass, a needle still in one hand and the fabric limp in the other. The large shirt and loose pants I was so eager to climb into a few hours ago now hang against my body like a sack, bits of thread stuck to everything in sight, including my hair.

"Damn."

"What?" My mother comes to the window, but by now Anthony Paul is on the front porch out of sight. "Who is it? Whose car?"

I pull a face without answering, dropping the fabric as the doorbell rings.

"It's for me," I say, thundering down the stairs.

Anthony Paul steps into the foyer without being asked. Very familiar. I look really bad and hope he can see me through the wrinkled, bedraggled clothes.

"I was waiting for you to call," he says as I point the way to the living room. "But you didn't and I guess I could have. But to avoid any possible ducking on your part, I decided an unscheduled visit was in order."

"You got a nerve," I say, sitting on the sofa. He sits next to me.

"Yeah, I know. My mother tried to whup it out of me, but she didn't have much luck."

"You musta made her real tired. You want a sip of something? Tea? Water? Orange juice?"

"No thanks."

My mother's light footsteps descend the attic stairs.

"Why'd you think I would duck?" I ask Anthony Paul.

"Just a feeling. Like I said, this way there's less chance of you saying no when I ask you out."

"You asking me out?"

"Yeah."

"That's a rather ass-backwards way to ask."

"All you have to do is answer. I'm thinking we'd go to Montgomery and see something at the Shakespeare Festival."

Anthony Paul has his back to the dining room so he doesn't see Mother poking her head tentatively around the corner. She makes an **O** with her lips before ducking back out of sight.

I smile. "Wow. A play? I haven't seen one of those since . . . well, a long time."

"I bet."

I frown at him. Insensitive Negro. But he is smiling and I can't help but be impressed by his sheer enthusiasm.

"So," I say. "When you want to do this thing?"

April 3, 1899

Mama say to me I try to hold on daughter cause I knew that ship had to hit land someday. Cant nobody be on the water forever. Aint natural. Someday it hit land and Id go home. Well jest about the time I think them ghost people could live on the water the day come and they led us out and throw sea water on us all and after I clear the water out my eyes I look out and the ship is beside a large wooden thing stuck out in the water. People everwhere but I thought I was going to fall down and die. I wasnt home. They was nothin but white ones far as the eye could see. Wimmin and chillun pointin and starin and lookin like ghosts. That was where they were pointin us to that land of walkin ghosts. Oh Joy I was dyin. I had to get off. I remember looking back cross the water and when I got close to the rail I climbed on top and the person next to me bump hisself on the edge of a rail. I was hangin there both feet over holdin the rail with my hands tryin to figure out how to jump without takin this other poor critter with me when one of them white men on the ship came and jerked me back. He got hold of the chain that was hooked to the chains on my wrists and pulled so that I fell back headfirst on the ship. I just lay there for a long time and the sores on my wrists open up again and I watched the blood run down onto the wood planks that soaked it up like the ship was thirsty. Drank it up. Drank it right up. A white man came and stood over me sayin somethin I dont to this day know what he said. And he stepped in the blood. When he walked away he made a bloody feetprint. The man chained aside of me grabbed me by the waist and helped me up cause the line was already movin gon into the land of ghosts.

I September 1980 — Tuskegee

really just want to know if something is wrong with me. Physically. I have to tell Daddy the whole story. But as soon as the words are out and I see his face, I remember Ruth's warning.

"Don't tell the doctor," she had said.

"You did what?" My father stares at me, his mouth twisted into a tight knot. He lowers the fountain pen he has been writing with at his desk. I stand before him like a guilty five-year-old. "When? Elizabeth . . ."

"I didn't know if something was . . . if I was sick or something. I thought I should check . . ."

"It's like that last time, isn't it?" he mumbles, not asking, but remembering. "Three years ago. I can't . . . you there on the floor staring up and not seeing anything. Talking to someone not there. Is it that again?" He looks angry and so frightened.

"No, not exactly. Sort of."

"Damn. Damn. Tell me," he mumbles, getting up from the leather chair behind the desk and coming to stand directly in front of where I sprawl on the small sofa in his study. I sit up abruptly.

"I was on a ship," I start, taking a big gulp of air. "A slave ship, Daddy."

He rubs his hand across his face, his buttery high-yellow skin turning a little paler.

"Maybe I was just sleepwalking," I continue. "But I don't know. I could see Ruth there, I just couldn't respond to her."

"Ruth saw this?"

"She pulled me out of the water."

"Elizabeth." He sits down next to me. "Have there been other episodes like this?"

"Well . . ."

"Tell me."

"I keep . . . winking out."

"Winking out? What does that mean?"

"Ahh . . . just, you know, sometimes it's like I get drowsy or just close my eyes and I'm not here anymore. I'm some other place."

"Dreams," he says matter-of-factly, letting out a sigh of relief. "You probably were just doing some crazy sleepwalking. Rare for someone your age, but not unheard of."

"I said *sometimes* it's like I get drowsy. Other times I'm just doing something else and I have a flashback of some moment or some place. I remember something that I know can't be true."

"Like . . . this slave ship?" His voice crumples under the word *slave* and he looks down at the floor, taking his glasses off for a moment, passing his hands over his eyes and replacing them.

"I've been there before," I say as quietly as I can—as if how I say the words can soften their meaning. "The moment is entirely real to me."

He gives me a disbelieving look but only says, "OK. What else?"

"I . . . sometimes have . . . pain after I come back." I rub my left wrist, remembering the angry welt that had been there. The wrist looks normal again, but a slight rawness remains.

"Pain?" That's a word that really gets his attention. He straightens his shoulders a bit and moves behind his desk again, fingering the cards in his Rolodex.

"Psychosomatic," he murmurs. "What is that guy's name?"

"Daddy?"

But he motions me to be quiet and a few moments later, he's describing my "symptoms" to someone I don't know.

Their voices, low and angry, are nevertheless quite clear; I feel as if the sound rattles the walls of our compact house. Mother swallows big mouthfuls of air between words, trying not to cry. But my father wears her out, the way he always does, with the weight of logic.

"If she's hurting herself, intentionally or not, I can't help her, Sarah," he says. There is a sound that, from where I stand just to the side of the closed study door, seems to be him opening and closing a heavy book.

"Visions—she says she's having visions of some kind. Has she said anything to you about it?"

"No, no, and John, I don't think this can be as bad as you say. I mean . . . a psychiatrist? You think she's crazy?" She rushes through her words in a whispery voice, excited, scared. "Sounds like a few bad dreams . . ."

"But she thinks they're more than dreams; that's what's dangerous, baby."

"Dangerous?!"

"She's having pains, she says. I can't let this progress. I have to stop it now."

Slumping a little against the wall and gently rubbing my wrists, I know, *I know* that I'm not crazy. But then, crazy people always know they aren't crazy. The irrational seems rational, right? The surreal seems real. So, maybe he's right and I need to go and have someone look inside my head. I shiver a little.

"Can't we wait?" Mother asks painfully.

"Wait for what, Sarah? For her to get worse? No, I've already called Daniels over in Montgomery."

"Daniels?"

"Psychiatrist friend of mine. He's good."

There is a long silence, and I slide down the wall to my own room. In the dresser's mirror, my eyes look very large, scary even to myself. How am I going to drown that expression from my eyes?

It's the hardest thing I've ever done in my life, getting into that car the next day beside my father's frowning body and watching the silence all the way to Montgomery and Dr. Daniels' office.

Turns out to be a quiet day, all the way around, though only on the surface. Under the skin, we all—John DuBose, Dr. Daniels and I—tend our little fires.

I leave Daddy in the waiting room when the nurse calls and I hope he'll be gone when I come out, if I ever do. But I know he'll be there. He'll have to question me after it's all over.

I have a waking nightmare that I am walking into the mouth of a hungry animal and will never be seen again.

My father picks up a magazine from the table as gentle, non-descript music floats on the air and I go through the door the woman holds open for me.

Dr. Daniels stands just inside. He has the largest feet I've ever seen; their size makes his white shoes look cartoonish. I keep my eyes on them as he stands back to let me inside his office and when I do look up I encounter his mild-looking, middle-aged brown face above his lab coat—also white.

He looks . . . comfortable. Easygoing. I relax my stiff shoulders, but I can't keep my hands from shaking, even when he begins talking in a low, conversational voice.

"Elizabeth," he says, gesturing to a chair in front of his desk. "I'm Charles Daniels. Have a seat, will you?"

He sits on the edge of the desk and folds his arms.

"You've been having bad dreams, I hear," he says calmly and a memory flashes of that ship, the rough wooden rail against my skin and the angry swirling water below.

I lick my lips, tasting salt, and try to fold my hands into one another so they won't move. *Don't let him see,* I think. *Just get through today without letting him see.* He says something; from the inquisitive look on his face, I guess he's asked me a question, but I don't exactly hear it. I tilt my head a little and pick up the end of his sentence.

" . . . finds these images disturbing."

"Excuse me? What?"

"I said, your father seems to find these images you describe rather disturbing. Can you tell me about them?"

"Yes," I say, taking a deep breath and lacing my fingers together. *Let him help you,* I say to myself. "Just a dream really. I guess. I mean, dreams. More than one."

"Just pick one and tell me about it."

Another deep breath and I plunge in. I tell him about walking along a dusty, faraway road, about Joy's button-up shoes, about Grace's bedroom that looks out on a sunlit pasture, about her children's smiles and her vague fears, about, most of all, stepping off the edge into nothingness, hoping to find water and rest.

In one long tumbling rush, I bring him to the ship's deck. Then he stops me.

"Back up," he says. "You mentioned this trunk. Tell me more about what was in it. A diary?"

"Yes, my great-grandmother Joy's diary."

"Um. And she wrote about this slave ship."

I know where he's going. My shoulders tighten.

"Yes," I say. "But—"

"The diary told the story of Joy's mother, who was African, you say?"

"Yeah. Mother and I read some of the diary after we opened the trunk. But when I had that first . . . dream . . . it was about something not in the diary. Even later, after I'd read the whole thing, I never saw that scene described. The one about my mother and I—not my real mother—walking down the road." I didn't tell him about waking up with dirty feet.

"It was a dream then?"

I stare at him, not knowing how to answer. I don't know what it was! I didn't know where I was—inside a dream or outside. He looks vaguely smug, satisfied, and I want to scream. I don't want to be here. My limbs lie heavy in the chair.

"It doesn't matter that your dream wasn't exactly like a scene in the diary. Reading about your African ancestor obviously put you in a certain frame of mind. We're all much more highly suggestible than we like to think. How long since you read that diary last?" he asks.

"Umm . . . four, five years, I guess."

"Now you know that everything we talk about is confidential. Everything. Even though your father and I are friends, you're my patient now and this all just stays between us. Understand?"

I nod.

"So," he says. "Is everything all right at home? Between you and your parents?"

I stare at him blankly for a full minute before realizing the suggestion.

"You think I'm reacting to something else? Something to do with my family?" I ask.

He sighs, unperching himself and going to sit in his desk chair. "It's not uncommon for someone to escape into their own world when things in the real world get traumatic," he says.

"If I wanted to escape, don't you think it would be to somewhere a little less horrible than a slave ship?"

He gives a little shrug. "The mind is funny that way, Elizabeth. It doesn't always work the way we think it should. The challenge is in finding out why you would want to escape to such a place. No arguments with your parents recently?"

"No." Could what he was saying be true?

"Boyfriend problems? Maybe something in the past you've pushed aside, perhaps because it hurts too much? It's OK to talk about anything here. You're safe to talk about it."

"But there's nothing to talk about," I say. "I can't think of anything like that."

"OK, Elizabeth" He sighs. "Think about it some more when you get home. And why don't you bring the diary in next time and we can read it together?"

"Next time?" I can't hide my distaste; I see it reflected in his wire-rimmed glasses and now somewhat stiff, dismissive smile.

"Yes. These things take time and care." He looks down at his desk calendar. "Next Tuesday. Two P.M." Daddy's already made the appointment for me.

"I can't bring the diary," I say. "It's too raggedy. It'll fall apart."

"Just read it again, then. Just reacquaint yourself with your great-great-grandmother's story. I think it'll help you start sorting out your life from the experiences that belong to other people, OK? We'll talk about it in detail next time."

"Why?"

"Just do as I ask. It'll help you sort things out, I promise. After that, we can talk about some other things."

"What other things?"

"Hold on, now." Again, that stiff smile. "One thing at a time."

I've never felt so trapped in my life. Except one other time. And there is no water here to cushion the fall.

" Y September 1995 — Montgomery

ou haven't asked me what I do yet."

"What you do?"

"You know, for a living."

"Are you a drug dealer?"

"No."

"A serial killer?"

"No."

"Cult leader?"

"Um, no."

"You hesitated on that one."

Laughter. "I know."

"OK, um, a snake handler?"

"No."

"Well, I can't think of anything else that would scare me enough to let go of your hand. Oh, yeah . . . psychiatrist?"

Now he really laughs, making the candle flames flutter. "Well, that's an idea . . . would it help me get inside your head?"

"Believe me," I say, looking down at the tablecloth for a moment, "many have ventured, but couldn't complete the journey, even after I opened the door and invited them inside."

"Ooo."

"Yeah. Anyway, I'm not ready to hear your life story yet, Anthony Paul, even if you're curious about mine. Don't let me talk about it. Just sit there and hold my hand."

"Yessum." He squeezes my fingers lightly, giving me a serene smile. His curiosity flows from his hand to mine. Perhaps the crazy girl is a novelty to him, some jones he's never had before. OK. I can live with that for now. Grace smiles from behind her past-life veil, and I relax in my chair.

"You didn't say much during the play," says Anthony Paul. "I thought it was good."

"Well, I guess I don't feel qualified to discuss drama," I answer. "I've never seen a real play before."

He nods. Of course. No need to ask why.

"Damn," I say softly.

"What?"

"I can't get away from it, can I?" I lean forward, smiling, wanting to live in the present for once.

"I know," he says gently, softly. "What are you going to do now?"

"Oh, shit, I don't know. My father asks me that, my shrink asks me that. You sure you're not a psychiatrist?"

"Aren't you a little curious about what I do for a living?"

"Mortician?" I raise his hand, pressing his palm against my lips. "Hmmm. No, no formaldehyde. Nice."

He laughs again, turning my hand over inside of his and kissing it.

May 17, 1899

One man there saw my arms and legs and the scars there and said somethin to the man what brung us off the boat Mama says.

Mama I say when was this.

The day they brung us off the boat she says rockin back a little in her chair. It was so quiet out there on the porch where we was sittin. Frank werent home, so there was not the usual sound of his stompin around. Her face looked tight.

We was in a space pen surrounded by walls like them courtyards I saw in Savannah she say. Still chained. But there werent nowhere to run to in that ghost land. I couldnt see where I was. Mama sighed real heavy then.

A man come and smear some bad smellin stuff on those raw sores on me. But it was a long time before they healed she say. She pull back the sleeve of her dress and looks down at her arms for a long time. The marks are there, old but true.

They goes with me when I go to God she say.

L October 1980 — Johnson Creek

ight comes so gently here among the trees. The first of day glows and grows through the windows of Aunt Mary Nell's room. Son Jackson sings just beyond the edge of the porch, where he's pulling dying plants from Aunt Eva's flower bed.

I've been in Johnson Creek three days with no dreams, no visions—not even a tingly feeling. Instead, I get up every morning and eat Aunt Eva's biscuits and blackberry jelly, just as I did when I was a child, and spend the day puttering around after her. And the end of the day finds me staring out at the blackness and straining to hear but finding the voices silent.

Son Jackson's song stops and I toss off the covers, pausing to finger the frame of the photo on the dresser before following the scent of coffee to the kitchen.

"You young," Aunt Eva says as I come in and plop down at the table. "You supposed to be up before me." She looks down at me over the top of her eyeglasses. "And you know you gotta be dressed before you sit down at my table."

"Good morning, Aunt Eva," I say, laughing and pushing my chair back to get up again.

"Good morning, baby. Put on some old stuff, hear?" I'm halfway down the hall. "We got to go over to the church today."

"I didn't know you still came in here," I say to her, watching her tie a clean white rag on her head. Inside the church, the pews squat in the dust like old folk praying and a family of dirt daubers buzz, out of broom range, around a window.

"You know, I'm not sure why I still come," says Aunt Eva. "Except that this place is one of the few things around here older than me. And even though there's no services here no more, somebody ought to take care of it." She pats her head idly and picks up a broom, indicating to me the other, larger, one. A push broom. "Sweep first. Then dust. Then . . ."

"Then?" I know I look appalled.

"Then"—she smiles—"polish and mop."

"There goes my vacation . . ."

Aunt Eva gives me a mock frown and I barely keep from laughing.

"Vacation?" she says, shaking her head. "What you doing taking a vacation in the middle of the school year? And is that what you came for? I thought it was something else."

My smile fading, I begin sweeping, trying not to think of the dismal efforts I've made at Tuskegee University this year. I have been so out of it, a few days without my morose presence in classes probably won't even register with my instructors.

Aunt Eva attacks a corner around the base of the pulpit with her own broom.

"Yes," she says. "After Mary Nell passed, I couldn't come in here at first. You know, we came in here all the time. Just couldn't let the place lie dead like that."

Letting the broom handle lean on a pew, I walk over to the pulpit and run my hand along the right side. Near the bottom, I feel a ridge, a scar. Bending to look, I laugh.

"There it is!" I almost yell.

"What? What, baby?"

"The heart. It's really here, just like you said."

She comes over to where I now kneel. My fingers trace the outline of a crudely carved heart, about as big as my palm. It has been polished many times, but the pulpit seems destined to be scarred forever.

"I didn't tell you 'bout no heart," she says, taking her glasses off and wiping the dust off before perching them on her nose again and peering at the pulpit. "I didn't know there was no heart."

"I guess it was Aunt Mary Nell, then. It was years and years ago."

"Mary Nell never told me about no heart. What's it say? It's got something carved in it. Well. Never saw that before, just polished right over it. I try not to bend down that far if I can help it."

"You said—or she said, I guess—that she carved her initials in it, hers and Uncle Henry's, when they were courtin'. "

"She told you that?"

"Somebody told me."

"Well . . ." She bends even further down, craning her neck. "Them initials there says . . . F. M. and J.W. That ain't Mary Nell's initials."

"Whose are they?"

"You sure Mary Nell told you about them? I know I ain't never seen them before. Didn't know to look."

"Um . . ." I stand up. "Her beau carved them one day while they were fixing the church . . . no, building the pulpit . . . he was working on it. But the preacher caught him and he got in trouble." I pick up the push broom again, wandering down one aisle and doing nothing more than raising the dust. "I was really . . . her mother was . . . upset. Didn't approve of the boy. She got in trouble too, it seems."

"Now, I know it couldn't have been Mary Nell and Henry. Mama thought he was gold," she says, a little too casually, I think. "Anyway, that pulpit was built before we was born." She snaps her fingers. "Where is my head? That could be Mother's initials! Frank Mobley. Joy Ward. That's about the right time, and I know he helped built some stuff around here. How cute! I wonder why she never told me about it?"

Aunt Eva chuckles to herself, running her fingers over the carving. I push dust, my heart beating much faster than it should.

"The past ain't never really gone, is it?" she says. "I'll give that old pulpit a extra polish today."

She hadn't known. Of course she knew. She's old. She just forgot she knew. Or she forgot Mary Nell knew and Mary Nell told me. Or maybe one of the twins—Frank or Phillip—had said something. My uncles are full of stories like that and know everything about everybody in Johnson Creek.

I turn the scenarios over and over in my mind, but something—something ancient and constant—tells me that I'm the only one on this side of death who knows anything about it.

An old vision—Joy and Frank and the inside of the church filled with working men—swims in front of my eyes, making them water, and I stop sweeping, waving dust from in front of my face.

"Whew!" I say in a shaky voice, "I should have brought a mask or scarf or something." Leaning the broom on a pew, I go over and attempt to open a window.

"Oh," says Aunt Eva, suddenly at my side. "These things are always sticky." She nudges me aside and opens the window on one try. I stare at the muscles that I've never noticed before in her arms. "There. Better. Why don't you get your air?"

Across the small stretch of grass, at the edge of the trees, a large cottontail nibbles warily. I breathe in, loudly, and the rabbit looks in our direction before darting back into the woods.

"Good thing Son Jackson wasn't here," Eva says. "He'd a shot it. That's probably the one that's been eating his cabbage."

"Yeah."

She puts her hand on my shoulder and crooks her neck to get a good look at my face. She smiles through her eyes, her lips in a serious straight line.

"One of these days, I'm gonna have to tell you about my parents," she says.

"What about them?"

"Well," she says, leaning her forearms on the dusty windowsill, "my daddy, Frank, was an Indian, you know . . ."

"Yes, I know." I sigh. Everybody's granddaddy or daddy or

mama's mama was an Indian. How many Indians could there have been, anyway? Then I caught a glimpse, in my mind's eye, of a young man with swinging black hair, laughing.

". . . and even though my grandmother had known him and his mother a long time, she was not happy when Mama took up with him. Mama used to laugh about how Grandmama kept after Frank Mobley to leave her daughter alone. But he was so doggone determined, he just kept hanging around and being polite and everything."

I smile a little, hearing, from far away, old Bessie fussing and fuming. "That boy done turned your head all around," she would have said in that funny accent of hers. "And we don't bit mo' know if he's worth somethin' or not. Looks worth nothin' to me. And I need for you to do better."

" 'You could do better,' Grandmama used to tell her," says Aunt Eva. "But Mama knew what she wanted."

Yes, that's what she would have said. I can hear her, that funny voice. Long dead before I was born, but still haunting my every present moment. *This is the wrong place to be,* I think, watching the oak tree branches bend to brush the tops of the tombstones in the old cemetery. *This can't be good for my . . . condition.* I turn my head slightly to get a glance of the pulpit just there, in the corner of my vision. I shouldn't have come here. What was I thinking?

The trees lean again in a slight wind outside, making the dappled sunlight move through the church. I try to stare out of the window at something, but there is nothing there except the same trees that have looked out over everything in Johnson Creek since time began. They know.

In the back of my vision I see the light moving near the pulpit. I close my eyes, feeling a slight sting. Tears. Aunt Eva still talks, looking out, while that frightening, familiar tightening of my chest muscles constricts my heart and quickens my breathing. I have to have known better than to come here. Where else would the visions of the past come but here?

By the time I open my eyes, I've already turned away from the open window. Matter of fact, I'm not standing by the window at all, but in the church doorway, fighting a feeling of both anger and resignation. Someone stands beside me, and in front of me Joy and Frank, clear as life, crouch near the pulpit, laughing.

It's just a moment. The person next to me says something in a sharp voice that I can't decipher and the two of them look up, startled and sheepish. I see the motion of their bodies in stages, like slow motion, and Frank's hair swings against Joy's cheek and she reaches up to brush it away from her face, caressing the lock briefly before letting it go.

I take a large step forward, but they are gone, and Aunt Eva has turned away from her contemplation at the window and is looking at me serenely as I stare at the old pulpit and the worn-down initials punctuated by dust.

"It's all right, baby," she says quietly. "I'm right here. You're right here."

"I can't get away," I whisper. "It follows me."

"What follows you, baby?"

"The past. Wherever I go."

She squeezes my arm and goes to gather the mops and brooms and rags and buckets. Hardly any work has been done.

"Come on. Come on back to the house and we'll fix dinner. We gotta talk."

Aunt Eva's knife slices the red-skin tomato into evenly thick pieces and she lays them on a plate, taking up a cucumber in almost the same motion. She begins carving cucumber rounds.

"Think of it like this," she says calmly. "The past—that's what you call it—is a circle. If you walk long enough, you catch up with yourself."

I start to laugh and go to the fridge to take out the cold fried chicken for lunch—or dinner, as she refers to the midday meal.

"Can't make progress that way," I say.

"But, well, think about it for a minute. Who better to tell you what's what than somebody who's already lived? And I'm telling you, baby, you done already been here. Well, I suppose almost all of us have been around once or twice. But you—you one of the lucky ones."

"Lucky?"

She goes on as if I've said nothing.

"They was strong-willed women, them two. Grace used to tell me about our grandmama Bessie. She knew everything about her. In the end, before she left to go up North, she knew she had already lived as Bessie. Ayo, Grace called her. Mary and me understood 'bout these things, but . . . everybody else woulda called her haunted or something, you know. It woulda scairt George outta his pants. No tellin' what he woulda done. We couldn't let it get out. But Grace didn't always have control over when or where Bessie might show up in her head. She went through a lot of what you're going through now."

"But what about the diary?"

"What about it?"

"Didn't Grace read Joy's diary, just like I did? She must have. How could she have been sure she wasn't just . . . dreaming about what she'd read?"

"Is that how it feels to you? Like you dreaming? Like you asleep?"

"Sometimes. I don't know." I sit down hard on the kitchen chair and put my face in my hands. "No. These days, I feel more awake than ever before. Too much."

"The diary, see, is just the key, baby. The diary. The quilt. Just the keys that unlock the door to what you call the past."

"So what are you telling me, Eva?" I watch her bustling from counter to table with cucumbers, tomatoes, chicken and cornbread, just reheated in the oven.

"I'm telling you, *Grace*"—I jump when she rather pointedly says my grandmother's name and realize that I'd left off the customary "Aunt" when addressing her—"that this time you have to control this thing, these memories, or you're going to be in trouble. And you can't pack your bags and run away from it. You gotta stick here with it."

Her tone is stern now and fear ripples through my body. I definitely felt something stir when she called me Grace. I watch her worn hands put out forks and napkins and feel trapped by the idea that this seventy-something woman is my sister. And my granddaughter. Oh, God, please.

"I don't know how to stop it," I bite out, trying to cover my terror with fake anger. "Control it?! This is crazy . . ." A storm falls on my face and I stand up now, crying in the cornbread. "I'm crazy, right, Aunt Eva? How did this happen? Was she crazy? Grace? It must run in the family . . . oh, no. No, no, no, no. I'm not letting this happen."

She just sits there, not looking at me, putting food on her plate and mine. She skips the cornbread.

"There's somewhere you need to go," she says.

"Where?"

"The house over on the other side of the creek."

I stiffen. "Grace's."

"Yes." She squirts hot sauce on her chicken. "Y'all used to play over there all the time. We had to fuss and fuss about being careful around all that falling-down lumber and old bricks. But you and Ruth used to run in and out of there. Play house. One of your favorite places." She looks at me, then back at her plate. "You been avoiding it."

Yes. Run. That seems my best choice right now. I sure as hell can't go over to Grace's house. The family still owns it and the twenty or so acres around there. Everything is so close here. This world, so small. It is maybe a mistake to have come to Johnson Creek. I need to go home and plan how to get away. Maybe I can convince my father that college in Atlanta is the cure for my failing grades and my odd behavior.

After we eat, Aunt Eva and I spent the rest of the afternoon on the front porch watching clouds gather. Back in Mary Nell's room, the iron bed creaks as I sit down on the edge. The night is not as gentle as it has been. It hangs heavy outside the window. There will be no sleep tonight. I might dream.

Things are all right for a couple of days. I don't have the energy to leave.

Aunt Eva doesn't mention what we talked about. I know she

wants to go back and finish up in the church, but I guess she also knows it will upset me, so she stays away. But the day after we have our conversation, I see Son Jackson creeping over there with a mop and bucket in the early morning hours. I have to smile about that.

I mope around the house for two days, though I do help Aunt Eva peel the last peaches for putting up and spend countless hours in her big garden, concentrating on burying my hands in weeds and dirt, falling in love all over again with the feel of mud. Sometimes I lie down between her rows of dying corn plants, the way Ruth and me used to when we were little, and become blue, just like the sky. Blue with whispers of white that flutter like wings and feathers.

Occasionally, Aunt Eva comes trotting out of the house and the tops of the corn rows ripple as she propels her old body through the plants, anxious because she can't see me. And she comes upon me lying there and I start laughing, because it's just like the old days, except Aunt Mary Nell isn't here and Ruth isn't here—Ruth, who can laugh louder than anybody. And Aunt Eva always sighs and purses her lips in mock anger before stomping back to the house. So for a minute, everything feels right, but only because I'm deep down in memory again— a more recent past thankfully, but I have to get out of the past or perish.

On one particular day I'm sure she comes crashing through the corn and gasps to find me gone. I don't know for sure. I have wandered over the shaky plank bridge that spans Johnson Creek and down the rutted, two-track red-dirt road that leads to Grace's house. I go even though I know I'm going to have one of those things, those episodes. I feel it coming long before

I leave the house and walk through the corn and over the creek and through the trees. I feel the mood of it, hazy and heavy, creeping up on me with every step.

That walk takes you back. Grace's and George's old property isn't far from the little cluster of homesteads that includes Aunt Eva's house, but the woods have always claimed it, and now the trees own it outright.

You would never mistake it for someone's home now. The window panes are gone. The porch and half the chimney have fallen off. The tin roof sags in the middle.

I can handle this, I tell myself as I slip up to the three-room house, going around to the back where steps still lead up to the kitchen door. Peering in, I see only a gloomy room, the house's furniture being long gone.

Ruth and I used to spread blankets in here and play. Then it seemed sunny and fun, our own playhouse. Now the trees are closer and the rooms darker. I sit down heavily on the top step, unable to go in.

It's so hard, I say silently, to anything, anyone that's there.

Ain't easy, Grace answers from somewhere down deep in my own head. *Nothing's easy.*

Leaning across the top step, I look again at the interior. My body is half inside the house already so I mentally shake myself and get up, dusting dirt off my hands.

There's nothing left in the kitchen but shelves and a few old iron pots, one of which still hangs in the fireplace. Several different varieties of vines grow through cracks in the walls, embracing the rotting wood with many arms and long green fingers.

The next room, I remember, was the children's room and the

next, Grace and George's bedroom. Then the house ends with
a window that used to look out over a field that had, at various
times, grown crops or livestock. I lean on the sill now, somehow
hoping to see cows crunching grass beyond the tumbledown
fence posts. I can still make out the opening where the gate
once was, but trees now obscure everything from the house to
the creek.

I still feel uneasy, but don't consider leaving until I find whatever Grace wants me to see.

"That's why I'm here, isn't it? Not to get away like I figured.

"I'm here to find . . . something . . ." I talk to the air, then climb
into the window, dangling one leg outside. It's about four in the
afternoon, and the air is cool and sweet, despite the anticipation
that hangs around the house.

And I wait.

Twilight. I can tell by the way the shadows have deepened in
the room. The floor digs into my butt. Damn. Why did I fall
asleep on the floor? That dust will be living permanently in my
clothes. I look down and notice, almost nonchalantly, that the
clothes are clean. And that they are not my clothes. Not my
shoes. Not my feet, legs or hands.

I am here.

I get slowly to my feet and go to the window, which has glass
panes now, and stands open. The sunset throws orange and
gold and pink across the bottom of the sky. Above that swirl of
color, stars speak of the night to come. I see it all without ob-
struction, because the trees I remember crowding the field beyond the fence have gone. Or rather, they have not yet arrived,
and all that crowds there are several dozen acres of rich grass.

A man's voice sings low, a song punctuated by admonishments to "get along there" and "go on now, I got to have my supper."

Yes, I smell it. Something. Cornbread, certainly, and something else familiar.

I look down at Grace's hands. I smooth those hands over Grace's dress, feeling awkward in the longish skirt, missing my jeans. This is a little different and odd. There is no merging, just an awareness of Grace, off to the side, doing the same things, sensing the same things I do. She moves closer. I keep looking over my shoulder, almost expecting to find her standing there with me. But she nudges me from the inside and I try to resist, to listen to her without becoming her.

But you're already here, she whispers. *This is your own self talking to you. Don't you understand? Ayo and me, we're here.*

A spasm of pain sears my back. I gasp, trying to keep my focus, and in that moment Grace steps forward and takes the blow. We stand there together in her battered body, bent double with pain.

The voice is George's. He's putting the mule up. He has been in the woods, cutting and dragging logs. The children aren't here today; they are up the road at their grandmother Joy's house.

Grace is restless. She's been fighting inside with memory. Ayo has been ever present, and Grace goes through the day crumpling under the weight of the old African's pain.

There will be no more hiding. By tomorrow, she will leave, taking her craziness with her. She's been looking for her suitcase, and she thinks maybe Mary Nell has it. But no, she gave it back. Can't be too far away in this little ole house.

"I gotta find that suitcase," she murmurs. This is the moment. She gets down on her knees and peers under the rather substantial iron bed. There are boxes and baskets under there, but no suitcase.

She rubs her wrists, watching the red marks grow and throb.

She sits on the bed, knowing she should get up and finish getting supper on the table. But she can't manage to move right now. She wants to find the suitcase before George comes in, and now she hears him wiping his feet on the kitchen steps. He's lifting the lid of the pot on the woodstove. The rocker creaks as he sits to take off his muddy boots.

She goes through to the children's room, opens the chifforobe and spots the suitcase on the top shelf. Closes the door as George comes in in his stocking feet.

"Smells good, baby, and I'm just 'bout ready. I'm gon' take a bath, though. Can you keep it warm till then?" He comes up and kisses her forehead and she feels a pang of regret.

"Sure."

While he heats his water, she goes back and drags the suitcase down. In their bedroom, she quietly opens dresser drawers and quickly, neatly, folds her best underwear and nightgown into the suitcase, pausing every few moments to slide a finger over her tear-wet cheeks.

George sings again as he dumps water in the tin tub on the porch. It is a love song, and she finally lets the tears fall freely, but doesn't slacken her pace. When the suitcase is full, she shuts it and slips it under the bed. Then, hearing him splashing and knowing he doesn't mess around in the tub too long when he's hungry, opens the trunk at the end of the bed, and empties its contents—a few towels, sheets, a tablecloth, an altar cloth that she keeps for the church—into the now-roomy dresser drawers. But at the bottom of the trunk is that quilt that she hasn't finished and the bag of cloth scraps she wants to use with it. She opens the bag and fingers the cloth, lingering over the precious bit of hand-dyed blue before putting it all back in the bottom of the trunk and going to get her dresses to stuff down on top. She puts in her three pairs of shoes. She has a photograph of herself and her sisters, smiling on Papa's porch. That goes in, along with a photograph of the children. There is no photo of George, but she won't forget him.

Water splashes outside as George unfolds himself from the tub. She closes the trunk quickly and goes into the kitchen.

When he comes in, she's spooning peas onto their plates.

"Good. I feel good," he says, coming up behind her and leaning to brush lips across the back of her neck. "Them young uns still at Mama's?"

"Yes." She walks over to put the plates down on the table. He shifts his body towards her. Where will he be when she leaves? In the field. She will walk to Cousin Janie's and her husband will drive her to Ft. Davis and the train. In the afternoon, when George is far beyond the trees. There will be no explanation. No note. What could she say?

"Even mo' good, huh?" he says, behind her again. And when she turns to go get the cornbread he locks her in a strong laughing hug, his face pressed into the curve of her neck.

Grace isn't ready for the pain. Her back is on fire. She tries to swallow the scream, but it bursts through, filling the house and the woods beyond. George immediately lets go, horrified, and she meets the floor with a dull thud.

"What did I do? Gracie? What did I do?" George kneels be-

side her writhing body, his hands reaching toward her in a gesture of helplessness.

She cannot answer; she can barely see his face through the
cloud of pain. He continues to talk, but there's no sound coming from his mouth. Someone else talks, soothingly singing.
She lies naked on her stomach, sobbing, as a gentle hand swabs
her back. The water in the pan grows darker in the firelight.
Waves of angry red slosh against the sides of the container. She
knows it's night. She knows where she is, but can't recall the
name of the place. A woman kneels beside the bed she lies in
and wipes her tears with the hem of an apron and Grace
reaches to touch her face. George's face appears there in her
place and then he too is gone.

I lie on the floor on my belly, my face in the dust. I can't seem
to move. Someone calls my name.

"Lizzie, where you? Where is you? Looord, where . . ."

It's dusk now, just like that moment long ago. Time's doorway remains open and Ayo and Grace have etched pain all over
my body. Had to go that way, I guess, but, damn, this whole
thing is getting a bit exhausting.

That's Son Jackson, out there calling my name. I guess Aunt
Eva sent him to find me. Yes, that's him stomping through the
house and exclaiming when he sees me sprawled on the dirty
floor of an abandoned house in the woods between no where
and no how.

Or maybe it's George, come back now that I can be forgiven.
Or Sam, who used to rock Old Bessie to sleep when the bad
dreams came and the sound of the ocean crept into her cabin,
but who was gone in the dark morning before the field boss

blew his horn. I close my eyes but the parade of images just continue to march in front of me.

Son Jackson doesn't say another word, just rolls me over and scoops me up, apologizing for my pain.

"I'm so sorry, little Lizzie," he says between my moans. "I'm a try to be gentle. Miz Eva say you might be hurtin'. "

Male arms, a mumbling in my ear and gentle cursing. "Shit, shit, shit," he says softly, stumbling for a moment with my considerable weight. But he's a strong-ass old man. I open my eyes and find that the stars have begun to move so so swiftly through the tops of the trees and over my nostrils drifts the scent of tobacco and sweat. Glancing back over Son Jackson's shoulder, I see Grace standing beside the house, her body bunched up in a protective stance. Futile effort against ghosts. Looking back like that through time, the night is a mirror.

N o v e m b e r   1 9 9 5 — T u s k e g e e

Anthony Paul is a printer and sometime artist, although I don't discover any of this until more than three dates out. And he isn't even the one who tells me. Sarah, taking his interest as evidence that I am returning to their world, figures out, quickly, that he's the same A. Paul that runs A. Paul Printing over by campus, and it's OK because his father is a Dr. Paul who works at the VA hospital and "knows your father."

"So," Sarah says, after she's beamingly relayed this information. "What's going on with you two?"

"Mother . . ." We're in the kitchen, and I try to turn my back on her and get back to washing dishes. "Just don't start to ask me everything all at once. I don't know the answer to that question. It may be a while before I know the answer."

"Well, something's going on . . ."

"Yeah. Something."

She releases a heavy, frustrated sigh and begins stacking pots. I look out the window, where I can see autumn seeping down past the horizon, the light leaving, the body of Earth rolling towards night. Father smokes a cigar in the twilight, in his lounger at the end of the brick patio.

The world turns and I have to get moving. Tuskegee, Johnson Creek, my parents' house—places I'm from but not where I'm going.

The shop is a fairly recent enterprise, Anthony Paul tells me; he moved back to Tuskegee a couple of years before, from New York. He lives in and is renovating the old house where he has his business.

We make love there for the first time amidst the dust and this seems appropriate; I'm always surrounded by dust, made of it, always caught up in it as it swirls and resettles and rises again and again to worry the living.

He's conquered a circular territory upstairs relatively free of debris and brimming with covered artist's canvases. He refuses to show me what's on them.

His bed is exactly in the middle of this space, a large, black-painted iron artifact that places the mattress so far off the floor that even our long legs dangle when we sit on it—and it's the only place to sit.

I laugh when I see it, thinking of the bed I once shared with George, not quite as ornate as this, but from the same era.

"What?" he asks, but I shake my head and continue to smile as he lights the dozen or so candles he has on the windowsills and floor.

My lips curve against his as he falls back with me on the quilt that covers his bed. "My grandmother made it," he says and I laugh again. He frowns confusedly at my amusement, but then laughs too, into my mouth, sending his breath through my body. He turns me toward him on my side, our chests fuse and his penis, hard and pushing against the fabric of his pants, sends a gloriously familiar jolt bouncing off the walls of my womb and up my spine. I slip my hands under his T-shirt. His body is hairless and smooth-skinned and rock hard, just the way I've pictured it, hoped for it, to be.

He begins unbuttoning my shirt.

"I don't know if we should do this," I say, jokingly, holding his hands away. He tries to use his teeth on the buttons instead.

"Why?" he mumbles.

"Once you get inside my body, you may want to get inside my head."

"Oh. Yes, definitely. I want to get in there," Anthony Paul says, abandoning the buttons and working on his own pants. "I'm just distracted with something else right now." He has a way of sounding urgent while conducting business in the most leisurely manner.

He kicks his pants off the bed. I raise my eyebrows at his lack of underwear. He pulls his T-shirt over his head and turns back to me.

"Do you want to stop?" he asks, a little too casually considering the size of his hard-on.

"No. But—things happen to people when they make love. You gotta realize that you'll begin to know me, and I'm not talking about just in the biblical sense."

"I already know you, old woman," he says, startling me. He

takes advantage of my momentary confusion to finish undoing my shirt. I haven't told him a thing about my past lives and yet here he is looking in my eyes with a knowledge so deep.

"Who are you?" I ask, the rush of sudden fear, overwhelming joy and sexual excitement stretching my lungs to bursting.

"It's all right, Lizzie," Anthony Paul says, making a cocoon of his arms and tucking me inside. He runs his fingers lightly across my back, tracing the scars' hard edges. "I'm just somebody who loves you."

Good answer.

I wake up because he's talking—no, singing—in his sleep, in my ear. I can't catch the words. Lying there, feeling human again after such a long time, I silently thank the gods that I'm here, alive and no longer celibate.

Throwing the covers off, I swing my legs out of the bed and go over to the window. Some of the candles are out, but the stars glow beyond the glass and I feel forever pressing down, even from where I stand.

I can't believe I'm going to get another chance to be loved after all those northern nights standing in front of windows facing south, missing everything, including the courage to go back. I see that time so clearly. Like yesterday. All the naked men in the world couldn't make love for me then, and I saw plenty of them, there in those factory ghettos so far away from Johnson Creek. Couldn't go back to George and make him do what he would have had to do. That would have broken us.

Anthony Paul moves on the bed and I hear him, feel him, coming up behind me. He sighs and kisses the back of my neck, then runs his tongue over the scars on my back, sliding his arms around me and covering my breasts with his hands. I lean back, tucking the top of my head under his chin.

"I know you," I say softly, half-hoping he won't hear me.

"Um-hmm." He turns me around and picks me up, kissing me hard. Am I in a movie? My legs fly everywhere; luckily there isn't far to go.

"I know you too," he says, sliding his hand between my legs. "I told you so. Just don't . . ." He stops and looks at me for a moment, before shaking his head and bending to lick a nipple.

"Don't . . . what?" I gasp a little as he opens his mouth, the soft skin of his inner lips damp against my breast, and sucks gently. I roll over on top of him, drawing the quilt up and covering us. I slide my hand between us and sink onto him, more sure than ever that I've loved him before. He lifts us both upward in one motion, his large hands digging into my skin, his mouth covering mine as he whispers, in a tone hanging somewhere between pleasure and sadness, "Don't ever leave me again."

May 18, 1899

I remember my fist being closed tight for what seem like years Mama say. I had a piece of cloth balled up in there. Beautiful blue cloth. But what I was wearin was just brown. Heavy stuff with all these folds. This in Savannah. My hands was tied up but I took that piece of balled up cloth with me to the block. It was a long time before I knowd what a pocket was. I be very po then. Thin you know. White man pulled me up there and I had my eyes shut tight and I heard laughin.

He put his hand in my mouth. Taste like dirt. He pulls my lips back and points to my mouth. My eyes open and I see all those ghosties lookin and pointin and talkin. I start to cry. Then he lifts the skirt of my dress with this walking stick he carrying. He lift it up up up and points. He say somethin, but I cant understand it I cant even hear. Just see him lips movin. I start cryin and moanin. I cant tell you the fear daughter. Fear. A scream starts creepin up in the back of my throat and I let it loose. They laughin laughin. Them strange people. And I scream and turn round and round in the same spot lookin for somewheres to go. But there aint none. I had a scream in me that go on for a hundred years. A black man hold the rope you know. The one tied round my wrists. And he lookin at me all pitiful like. Sorrowful like. And I say to him baba father take me home. This place is not for us. But he just look at me and then at his feet.

October 1980 — Tuskegee

Two days after my visit to Grace's house, Mother fetches
me, hardly sitting down for a glass of Aunt Eva's lemonade
before hustling me to the car and down the road. I wince a
bit on the way to Tuskegee, not only from the unholy pain in
my back, but from my mother's nervous glances and inat-
tentive driving.

"There's something there in the road, Mother," I say, as she
rounds a country curve, looking at me instead of Highway 29.

"I see it!" she snaps, turning back to the windshield just in
time to veer to the right and miss the startled animal—a small
skunk—that rests on the center line. "You don't have to tell me
how to drive," she says.

"Where's Daddy?" I ask.

"It's Saturday, you know. He's golfing with the guys down in Montgomery. He was already gone when Aunt Eva called."

"Sure." I shift in my seat, grimacing, but glad to notice that my back feels better, less raw.

"What on earth have you been doing . . . I mean, what's wrong? Did you fall or something?" she asks.

"No, not really . . ."

"I mean," she continues without letting me go on, which is good, since I have no idea what to tell her anyway, "when Aunt Eva called she said you weren't feeling well. 'She needs her mama,' that's what she said to me." She glances over at me in anticipation, but I don't offer anything so she goes on. "I'm glad you got to spend some time with your great-aunt; she's lonely without Mary Nell and really shouldn't be down there by herself. One day Pat is going to have to decide what to do about that. She talks sometimes about moving back to Johnson Creek permanently to be with her mother. Can't let Aunt Eva rattle around in that old house by herself . . ."

And she's off. Nervousness. She'll chatter all the way home. The tires whisper along the road in strange syncopation with her words. Somewhere between Smut Eye and Union Springs, she takes a breath and looks over at my face, which is partly pressed against the window.

"Are you sure you're all right?" she asks. "You're not having bad dreams still?"

No. Yes. You have no idea, I want to say. I want to spit it out, growl at her, even though I know it'll frighten her. Something terrible is happening to me. Can't you tell? But when I turn to answer her, some part of me still knows I can bear the fear more than she can.

"I'm just tired," I say instead.

Just like at Aunt Eva's, the first few nights are fine. The pain in my back fades. I call Ruth and ask her to send me the Spelman College catalog, though I don't know how I think I'm going to transfer in with those grades from Tuskegee. Maybe I can start over, pretend like I've never been to college before and just use my high school grades.

Things seem almost normal for a minute, with autumn just creeping along; I can almost push Grace away—away back in my mind. I note almost absently that the other one hasn't appeared in my "visions" lately—Bessie, or Ayo, as she likes to call herself. But besides that stray thought, I feel relatively carefree for at least three or four days after coming back from Aunt Eva's.

Until Daddy reminds me I have missed several appointments with Dr. Daniels; his secretary has been calling.

"I'm serious about you going, Elizabeth," he says one night after dinner when we're sitting in the living room. "One session isn't going to fix it—"

I wonder if he knows what "it" is. I know I don't.

"—and I know something happened down at Eva's. You can't hide that from me."

I look away from him without saying anything and meet Grace's melancholy stare from the faded photograph on the wall.

"I know you're listening to me," he continues in the deep, tight tone that he uses to awe me.

"Yes."

"Good. Then I can count on you to call Daniels' office to-morrow and make another appointment. I don't have to stand over you and make you do this, right?"

"Yes, OK."

Daniels wants to talk about Joy's diary. *What a way to spend a sunny day,* I think, sitting there with my hands on my knees, looking at him looking at me.

He hints that my "episodes" are glorified dreams that grew out of my romanticizing of my great-grandmother's writings. A fanciful, imaginative little girl, that's how he sees me. Even now, he half-smiles as he suggests we dissect and analyze all the scenes I have tried to describe. It's so hard to make him understand the enormity of what I have felt, and of what I feel approaching.

He wants to talk about the diary; instead I talk about my visit to Johnson Creek.

"I saw my husband," I say.

"You don't have a husband."

"I did." I get up from the chair in front of the desk where he sits and walk slowly around the room.

"Your husband. What's his name?"

"George." I smile as I remember his face. "George Lancaster."

"And what does he look like?"

"Oh. Fine. Very fine. Tall. Our kids are bound to come out like giants. The twins are already looking like little trees."

"Twins?" I hear a catch in Daniels' questioning voice.

"Well, three children altogether. Twin boys. I didn't see them

this time. Just George. And Son Jackson. And Grace . . . I saw
Grace standing there by the steps. She was cold . . ." I trail off,
confused a little.

"I thought you said you were Grace," Daniels says.

"I am. I can see her and I can see through her. I remember
what her body feels like. And both of us, me and her, are sort of
superimposed on another person."

"And that would be . . . ?"

"That's Ayo. Bessie. I don't always remember her too clearly.
She's too far away." I rub the fingers of my right hand over my
left wrist. There's a faint, reddish mark there, and another on
my other arm. "You see that?" I turn and thrust my hands toward the doctor, leaning over the desk. "What is that? Those
marks?"

"I don't know, Elizabeth. Perhaps you scratched—"

"I didn't! I didn't!" And then there's my back, and the rawness that's faded to a throbbing and now a slight soreness that
I feel when I sit back down in the chair. I can't bring myself to tell
him about all that. "Look at them," I say, laying my wrists in
front of me on my lap. "They're perfectly round, those marks."

He doesn't say anything and I just sit there, breathing hard,
trying to . . . I didn't know . . . trying to stay sane.

"You don't know anything," I say after a few minutes. "You
have no idea what you're dealing with, do you?"

"I really believe you're just having a very elaborate fantasy
about your ancestors. It's not necessarily a bad thing to imagine what their lives might have been like, but Elizabeth, you
can't lose yourself in those old stories. You obviously are using
them to fill some emptiness in your life. You've got to find out
what that is."

"Oh, bullshit," I say, my voice barely above a whisper. "I'm not trying to fill my life. This is my life. These people belong to me. They . . . it's like they've always been there, trying to make me hear them."

"Are you saying you hear voices? Is there some kind of voice in your head trying to tell you to do something?"

"No, no, no, no!" I slump down in the chair, scowling at him.

"Go on," he says. "What do the voices say?"

"There are no voices, Doctor," I say flatly. "What I'm trying to tell you is that these are memories, that's what they feel like. And when the . . . conditions, I guess . . . are right, they're more than memory, they're events. They're replays of things that have already happened. Do you understand? I'm there, I see things, I hear things, I feel everything that's going on."

"Elizabeth," he says quietly, leaning across the desk. "Don't get angry. But truthfully, don't you think they might just be dreams?"

"Truthfully? No. I don't think they're dreams. But why don't we just admit—you and me—that we don't know what's going on?"

Daniels won't answer for a moment; he just makes his notes. Finally, he hands me a small piece of paper over the desk.

"These should help you sleep," he says. "Calm those dreams."

"You just don't get it," I say tightly, crumpling the prescription in my fist.

"Just take them," he answers gently. "And make another appointment with my secretary. I'd like to see you a week from now."

Daniels gives me sleeping pills, because, he said, he is convinced I am having some sort of "super-sensitive dream disturbances" and a few nights of uninterrupted rest might break the pattern.

My gut tells me he's wrong, but just in case I take the pills out before bed that night, intending to take them.

Mother comes in without knocking, sees them on the nightstand.

"Oh, did the . . . doctor . . . give you these?" She picks up the bottle. I'm pin-curling my hair and in the mirror I see her examining the label.

"Yes," I say, half-hoping that she'll offer some objection. But, true to form and true to her all-out fear and respect of doctors, she does not.

She simply puts the bottle back and says casually, "Those are good. They'll put you right out. You probably need the rest."

She's just confirmed a long-held suspicion I've had. So that's what is in some of the many bottles that she keeps arranged neatly in her dresser drawer.

"I made that hair appointment for you," she says, at the door. "Next Thursday? That won't conflict with your doctor's appointment, will it?"

"No." I wasn't planning on going.

"OK. Good. Try to get some rest."

I shake my head as she closes the door behind her, feeling incredibly alone. The visions don't really scare me anymore. I expect them. I've grown comfortable when I'm inside them. But in the world I am supposed to know, I feel as if a trap is slowly being sprung.

A blue bandanna goes on over the curls. I stop to adjust it; my memory gropes for something, something about this moment. After sitting there through a few heartbeats, straining to find the thought, I give up and sit on the bed. I pick up the pill bottle, trace a finger over the typewritten words on the label, then open the drawer of the bedside table and drop it in.

No. If I'm going to go around in a fog, it'll be one of my own making. I'm not going to run from "it" anymore—as if I ever could.

Sleep is surprisingly easy. Sometime in the night, I wake and find that the bandanna has slipped off. Turning on the light, I retrieve it from under the pillow and start tying it back on. Catching a glimpse of myself in the mirror, I freeze for a moment, tight, then relax. Another girl looks back at me from the mirror. Fifteen, maybe. I've never seen her before but I know her. Someone I can't see is tying a piece of dark blue cloth on the girl's head. I can't see the other person, just a pair of large brown hands. I can't tell if they are male or female hands. The girl looks confused; her confusion goes right through me. I sink back down into the bed, turn off the light.

That's what it's like for the next few days. I know their names. The girl is the young Bessie. In her mind, she still calls herself Ayo. I hear her talking to herself and she's in the mirror a lot, always doing something other than what I'm doing. Other times, she walks with me, so close behind that it's as if she steps on the backs of my shoes. I often turn to look over my shoulder, but she is not flesh; she's a shadow on my heart.

Even before realizing the girl's name, some part of me knows I'm delving into a more distant past then those moments I spend in Grace's world. I'm a little farther away from Ayo, but glad to be. Sadness, an ever-present ache in her chest, crushes her. Sometimes I'm doing some ordinary little thing, and I get that tightness in the chest and throat as if I'm holding back a flood of tears and Ayo is there in my memory, crying and lonely, trying to tell me of some long-ago hurt. I spend entire days on the verge of tears.

One night at dinner, *that* night as a matter of fact, I'm trying to decide if I want another roll and water splashes on my plate. Quickly, I put the napkin up to my face, but Daddy has seen that I am crying.

"What is it?" he demands.

"Nothing," I whisper fiercely. They've been watching my melancholia grow as the days pass. Mother tries to take me out—on shopping trips or to club meetings—to escape the thickly sorrowful air that seems to be suffocating us all. But I'm afraid to go, afraid I'll lose my grip in front of her friends.

"I'm all right," I say now.

They both stare at me in speechless wonder, I guess because my voice sounds perfectly calm, almost bland, but the tears fall like rain.

"I'm finished," I say, standing quickly and sweeping my plate, napkin and glass up. Before another comment can be made, I am in the kitchen, running water in the sink. The clock on the stove tells me it's barely past seven. Should I retreat to my room now, as I've been doing for the past few nights? It's probably better that way. No looks. No questions. No stilted conversation.

I'm combing and rolling my hair at the dresser and Little Ayo is at our window, the mirror. She looks at me with my own eyes, wet with tears. Her mouth makes words I cannot hear. I know her face well by now and I don't move because if I look away she'll be gone.

Today she's dressed in the blue cloth, decorated with lively patterns in white, her head wrapped in matching fabric. She looks beautiful, but her face is all pain. A huge sobbing cry gathers itself behind my eyeballs, but I keep combing without letting it loose.

For hours, it seems, we sit there. I've finished my hair, but still clutch the comb; I can't get up and let her go. She gestures, and I watch her touch her clothing, unable to see anything but the raw scars on her wrists, rings of fire. I feel my own fingers move, and slide my right hand over my shirt at the waist. That blue-dyed African cloth I'm looking at in the mirror seems to fold right under my fingertips, its satiny feel surprising me. *It's that indigo dye, beaten right into the cloth,* says something from somewhere deep. *Our mother made this. She is a master dyer.*

Blood begins to ooze from Ayo's wounds and my comb falls on the carpet with a soft thud as I grasp my wrists, trying to contain the pain. I jump from the chair with a muffled yelp and stagger back against the bed. As I fall, the colorful pictures on the quilt's surface rise up to greet me.

I sit up for a moment after lying there for I don't know how long. Not asleep exactly, just away. I turn out the light and let the moon take over. I wiggle out of my clothing and lie on top of the bed in my underwear, much too aware of the steady pain that grapples with my body and my will. My back is no good, so I turn onto my stomach, cheek nestled against the raised pattern of the quilt, arms dangling over the sides of the bed. The bottle of sleeping pills rests at eye level on the nightstand. I prop myself up just long enough to down two capsules, dry.

Well, says Grace, in an almost mocking tone. *We was back there. There in that ole house back up in them woods. That there was the night, baby chile, that almost did me in.*

"Yeah," I think, trying to focus through the pill-induced haze. Laughter wells inside; Grace giggling. I don't hear her, really. Just her thoughts, snaking between my own.

Yeah, she continues, *that Ayo, she rushed in without warning and there I am flat on my back, wiping up blood from some old wound from some dead time. She's all pain, my grandmother. What I have of her is all pain. That night George touched me and she was there, reeling from some beating she had long before I was born. Whew! I didn't understand it all then. That's why I was going, getting out. Packing my bags and shakin' off that Johnson Creek dust. And that wasn't the half of it. . . .*

"Too fast," I say silently, foggily.

You mean too late. Your time here just like it was for me that night. I scared George to death, she said. *When I asked him to bed down by the fireplace, he didn't argue. Later I was in bed, unable to sleep and in pain, trying not to scream out. And the pain just got worse and worse and then I was . . .*

"On the ship?" I ask, watching the scene unfold inside my closed lids.

On the ship. Couldn't get off. Water everywhere. Lord, I wanted to jump. I seen myself falling down into the ocean, but it was too late, really. Time for that kind of escape had done passed. So they drug me off

and everywhere that iron chain touched me blood ran like a river,
down my arms and ankles and . . .

"Onto the deck of the ship," I whisper, sitting up in bed. I
know my eyes are wide and staring; the tepid warmth of the
moonlight sneaks in the bedroom window, but the room is fea-
tureless. It's dark for a moment and then, miraculously, there's
sunlight and cool salty air and—raw, unapologetic pain.

You see? Grace says matter-of-factly as I give up and let loose
a stabbing scream. *You can't sit still for that kind of thing. I had*
to go.

Blood drowns everything. Blood and water and brown bodies falling down and never landing.

I watch red drops seep through my skin, onto the quilt, onto
the carpet, but I have no astonishment left.

The moonlight filters slowly back in. I sit ramrod straight,
sweaty and slick. Prince stares down disdainfully at me. Grace
and Ayo are gone and the pale glow coming through the window draws a sharp picture of the horror on my mother Sarah's
face. I don't remember her coming in, but she's there shaking
me, crying and calling my name.

"Lizzie! Oh, Lord, oh, Lord! John!"

The switch clicks and the overhead light comes on, hard and
utterly real. Daddy lets out a mangled yell. The front of my
mother's pale yellow, satin nightgown is soaked, red and wet.
"Call the ambulance!" she screams at him and he staggers out.

"Sarah, Sarah . . ." I reach out and touch her face. "I had to go.
I had to. . . . But I didn't forget you. I never forgot you. I can explain." Torn flesh at my wrists leaves a smear of blood on her
cheek.

"What have you done?! What have you done?!" Sarah screeches. She puts her arm around me to lift me and the scream leaves my throat even before the pain gathers its strength and ricochets inside my brain. She takes her hands away from my back and stares at the blood on her hands. "Lizzie . . ."

What have I done? All the aches and mysterious stabs of pain now have their corresponding wounds. Raggedy, ugly, familiar skin openings and welted patterns. I put my right hand to the opposite wrist and try to put the skin back together, twisting my body so as not to stain anything further. A futile move. There is an already-drying pool of blood on the quilt, right across, soaking into, Ayo's face. Round, red patches careened across the carpet like drunken stepping stones. Have I been up?

Daddy lurches back into the room, carrying his medical bag, towels, a pan of water.

"Oh, God, Lizzie," he rasps. He sits behind me. "How did you do this? Oh, damn . . . you have to be stitched . . ."

"Daddy," I say, smiling, then grimacing as he gingerly swabs at the blood on my back, "I can go back in time . . ."

I watch the water in the pan make red waves.

November 1995 — Tuskegee

"There's something so beautiful about it," Anthony Paul says, following the raised pattern on my back with his fingertips like a blind man trying to read a horror story. "Gut-wrenching to look at. But so beautiful it's hard to stop looking."

His voice startles me out of my contemplation of the large covered canvas opposite the bed. I thought he was asleep, thought I heard gentle snoring from where his mouth pressed against the skin behind my ear as we nestled together on our sides.

I reach for my shirt, which landed on the floor sometime during our first or second—or third—lovemaking session. He tries to stop me from sitting up to put it on.

"You weren't worried about me seeing those a few hours ago," he says.

A few hours ago, I wasn't thinking about trying to explain those scars.

"You . . . you don't even seem to be startled by them," I say, managing to pull the shirt over my slightly trembling body.

"Well, I was. Though maybe not for the reason you think. Just another thing to discover about you, Lizzie," he says. "I'm looking forward to hearing all about it, but I can wait until you're ready."

I press my feet to the floor, walking away from the bed, trying to explain to myself how, after all I've been through, I can still feel fear.

The large covered canvas is in front of me, and I put my hand on top of it, leaning there for a moment. It's the biggest canvas in a room filled with ghostly rectangular beings propped on windowsills and against doors. This one covers the entire wall it leans on.

Maybe it's because I feel Anthony Paul watching me from the bed, waiting for a response. Maybe it's because I need a diversion. I don't know why I decide to snatch the cover off that canvas. But what I see when I do makes me almost fall over.

She steps out of a swirl of water—the ocean, obviously, in the midst of a storm. A girl-woman walking into the unknown. In the distance, the waves toss a ship. She is obviously nude underneath a cloth that is wrapped around the waist of her slight body. She has her back to us—a back crisscrossed with a lacy pattern of scars—but looks over her shoulder directly into my eyes.

In the old days, this kind of thing would have sent me reeling backwards to some other place and time. Instead I take a few steps forward, pulled in by her eyes.

"It wasn't from school," Anthony Paul says rather jerkily as I shuffle closer to the painting, putting one finger on it, on the beautiful blue fabric that he has so lovingly draped around her. "It wasn't from school that I knew you. It was from this. Look at her face."

I am looking. It's mine. It's my face, a mask of shock and anguish. My eyes slide to the date scribbled in the corner. January 1982. While I lay silent and wandering, immersed in past dreams at Bentwood, a young man was putting layer upon layer of my past on this canvas. This sacred cloth.

"Lizzie?" He watches me stumble back until my knees hit the bed and I sit down abruptly, making it squeak. "It is you . . . isn't it?"

"Yes," I say, frowning. He sits up beside me, but I get up immediately and start fumbling around on the bed for my underwear.

"This was one of my first big pieces," he says, watching me frantically toss the covers. "I did it years ago. I don't remember where the image came from. A dream maybe?"

A dream. I shake my head, my eyes wandering back to the canvas.

That's what they used to call the things I saw and heard and felt. Dreams. I know it's more than that. How much should I tell him?

I walk over and touch the place where she wears her shackles. He already knows more than he thinks.

"Maybe," I say. "That's . . . astounding. Beautiful." I turn back to him and smile slightly. "You really should think about

showing your work. I don't know why you're hesitating." He
looks at me quietly, knowing that I'm hiding.

"I think," I say, leaning over his body and pulling my pants
out from where they've somehow become wedged between the
mattress and box spring, "I should get home. Mother . . . she'll
be waiting up."

"Do you want me to take you home?" he asks, catching my
hand. "You can get your car later."

"That's all right. I'm fine." I squeeze his fingers and brush his
lips with a kiss. "I better go. She'll be worried."

I leave him sitting on the edge of the bed, looking abandoned.

I don't know how I manage to get home with the image of
that painting bouncing around in my head. Luckily the house
is dark and quiet when I get there, because if Mother had been
up to question me about my date, I doubt if I would have been
able to form a coherent sentence.

Of course morning comes, but by the time Mother is hound-
ing me over breakfast about my evening out with Anthony
Paul, my feelings have become a bit easier to hide.

"You were out a long time," she says, pouring coffee into my
father's cup.

"She tried to wait up for you," Daddy says. "I keep telling her
that Anthony is all right."

"I'm sure he is, John, but . . ."

"Mother," I interrupt, "there was the movie and we had a
long dinner afterwards. And then we just got into a big discussion . . . time just got away from us."

She sits down and begins spooning scrambled eggs onto my
plate, smiling. "You look so cute together," she says. "I don't

mean to sound like a worrier, Lizzie, but you know you don't have the experience with men that most women your age do. I mean, most likely you'd be married by now if . . . if things had been different."

I sigh and Daddy makes that his cue to leave for his regular Saturday golf game.

"You going to the hardware store today?" Mother asks.

"No. Uncle Frank and Uncle Phillip have me on a Monday-through-Friday schedule." I had just begun working that week, at the front counter of my uncles' business. It is a whole different brand of boredom and every day while I sit there all I think about is getting back to making the new quilt.

I have decided that this is the day. The quilt pieces are all sketched out in colored pencil. After breakfast I very deliberately lay all nine drawings out on the dining room table for Mother to see, from the first circle—a picture of Grace in her house packing her trunk—to the last—a glorious funeral with the woman's spirit hovering nearby.

"All right, it's gonna be like a horseshoe," I say, laying two completed blocks on top of the corresponding sketches, "and we've finished these three patches already." There's one of Grace reaching for the moon. There's the trunk-packing picture and another of Grace boarding a train.

Mother smiles at me rather tentatively. "I guess some of this family's traditions rubbed off on you after all." She runs her hands over the blocks. "They are beautiful," she says, smiling a little wider. I'm happy with the change in her during the past year I've been home. The withdrawn, worried woman who came so often to the hospital to visit is gone. Her smile these days reminds me of the child, the little girl from Johnson Creek I left behind.

"Wait until your Aunt Alene sees it," she says.

"Whoa! It's too far from finished."

"But she'd like it. Why don't you take these blocks down to the store with you? She's still in there every day, right?"

"Yeah. I get the feeling that Uncle Frank won't let her out of his sight for long. He still thinks she's the most beautiful woman in the world." I pause, looking at her closely. "Except for his mother, of course."

"Yes." Sarah laughs. "Love among the screwdrivers. They are real cute, those two."

"And he has all those old photos up in the store from Aunt Alene's singing days. Not to mention their kids. Gray, Eddie, Billie."

"There are some real beautiful women in our family, that's for sure. Alene still. And Billie, unmistakably. Come to think of it, she has a look about her . . ."

"She looks a little like Grace—Grandmama—don't you think?"

Her head is bent over the quilt pieces and she picks up one, running her fingers over the seams. "Yes, I suppose. From the pictures, I mean. I don't really remember her face myself. Well, sometimes I think I do. Sometimes I think . . ."

"You think what?" I feign nonchalance, slowly circling the table, collecting the drawings and sticking them into the back of my sketchbook.

"I think . . ." She drops the circles of cloth and goes over to the doorway between the dining and living rooms, staring silently for a moment at Grace's picture on the wall, the one where she sits so pensively in her white dress. "I think I remember her voice. She's been on my mind a lot lately. She was quite a person."

"Yes, she was." I stack all the papers and cloth together on the table. She turns and looks at me, frowning uncertainly. " . . . from what I hear," I add quickly.

"I wish you had known her. I wish *I* had known her. I don't know why she's been on my mind so much," Sarah says, going all the way into the living room now and staring eye-to-eye with the photograph.

I come into the room, standing behind her, marveling again— for the first time in a long time—at the forces that have brought me to stand here with a clear view of the past and the present and the marriage of both.

"Every woman needs her mother," I say now, putting my hand on Sarah's shoulder.

She turns, laughing nervously. "Oh, you sound so wise and matronly." Then her smile fades. "I just hope I haven't failed you," she says. "I used to think that, you know. Sometimes I still do. I wonder about the woman you could have been, if all this hadn't happened, and maybe, I think, I didn't do something. My mother wasn't there to teach me, so maybe I didn't know how to do it right."

"I am the woman I should have been, Mother, the woman I was meant to be." I grab her by both shoulders now, bending a little to look right into her face. "If you're still thinking you did something, or you didn't do something, you're only messing with your mind. You didn't have anything to do with what happened to me. Believe me, Mother. You had nothing to do with it. OK? If anything, it's what's been done to you that's not fair." I straighten, dropping my hands and closing my eyes for a moment to shut out her worried expression. It's been so good lately, I don't want her to hurt anymore. All those times in the hospital when I was sarcastic to her—just mean and scared—I regret now. That was just adding insult to injury.

"I'm sorry," I say.

"For what?" she asks. I open my eyes and she's frowning at me. I just smile, shaking my head.

"For everything," I say. "For being so mean to you and Daddy. For being so distant."

"Oh, baby." Now she reaches for me and places her palm against my cheek. "I know it wasn't your fault; you were sick. We know you had no control over what happened to you. We understand that."

"I don't want you to ever worry about me," I say. "I wouldn't change anything. I feel like I had to go through it all to be safe."

"Safe?"

"From fear. There's not much that frightens me anymore."

"I wish I could say the same."

"Maybe you will be able to someday."

She shakes her head, walking into the dining room to gather up the stack of materials. "I'm not as strong as you, baby."

"Yes, you are," I whisper as she leaves the room to climb the ladder to the attic. "Yes you are. I'll make sure you are."

October 1, 1899

I went to Atlanta back of a big wagon with four other slaves. I was so worn out and scared I couldnt talk. And nobody understood me noway. The people what bought us was two white mens. They didnt say nothin to us except to yell when we said a word. There was two men slaves that tried to talk. Think they knew each other. And there was a woman. And a little girl child. I could tell she werent not her mother but she held that baby hand anyway. The woman kept pointin to my head and sayin somethin. Her hair was covered up with a dirty cloth and I thought about my mamas beautiful died cloths wrapped around the womens heads like crowns. I put a hand to my chest where I had that piece of blue cloth from home rite there next to my heart under the clothes. The woman point to her head again and I touched my naked hair wantin to cry.

You understand baby I didnt know then where I was, where I was going. I was just like a sack of meal you know. Loaded up and toted from place to place. We got there at Atlanta and spent the night in a little room with bars. I heard all kinds of noise outside. Horses and wagons and thangs and people shoutin. Real busy place. I couldnt sleep good on account of those scars and every time I did drop off I felt that water rollin underneath me like I was still on that ship. She sigh deep rite here put her sewin down on her lap for a minute. Then she say I cant tell you how I miss dem though I knowed they long gone now over there. Mama papa. I wish I could remember they names.

18

November 1980 — Montgomery

Daddy tries to sew me up that night, but his hands shake and he waits for the emergency guys to do it. He just ends up hovering. I remember seeing him reflected in the dresser mirror, breathing heavily, his whole body rigid with disbelief. Mother is standing in the corner of my room by this time, sobbing and horrified. And while the paramedics sew and bandage, Daddy keeps screaming at me to tell him what I used. A knife, a razor, what?

But by this time, I can't say anything. I have no control. My body jerks and they're trying to stick me with things. They hang up a bag of blood, somebody gives me a shot and I wake up at Bentwood in a room locked from the outside.

During the two years of silence, I dream memories of Africa

every night and wake to mornings of fiery pain. My scars burn at the edges.

In those first moments of consciousness, when the light glows weakly through closed lids, the scent of home is all around. Soft, damp leaves. Wood fires. The dusty odor of bare feet on the road, the road to the town and the market. It's not only the smell of a different land, but of a different shore and an elder time. A childhood memory. The notes of my mother's traveling song and the rhythm of her steps cling to me, like sweat.

Surely, if they knew, if they heard and smelled and saw all, they'd understand how speech, for me, has become inadequate.

Dawn always brings me back, at least for a while. Inevitably, my eyes open and I'm momentarily blinded by the blond blandness of the narrow room, which is just the right shape for the narrow bed on which I lie immersed in some mental state that only I, in time, will ever understand. And then, the nurse is coming down the hall, insisting that I get on with my face-washing and teeth-brushing or I won't be getting breakfast on time.

My father will never know how much he assisted me by choosing Bentwood, where the almost incessant clamor of diseased minds whispering and doctors consulting and nurses baby-talking make my silence a personal haven. I create space inside all that chatter for all the lifetimes I didn't know I had, the ones I couldn't tell him about when they were loading me into the ambulance the night the blood came.

The hospital isn't too bad really, although six months pass before they let me out for more than a piss and a scrub. Even

Grace thinks it isn't so bad, though this is the kind of place she feared the most, the kind of place she fled from. Of course, she reminds me, in those days she would have gone to a bona fide asylum. This ain't so bad, she thinks, despite the bars and locks and the constant watching of every move and bodily function. If only that white doctor man would leave us alone.

No one here understands the necessity of silence. Sometimes, as I sit outside on the grass listening, doctors walk by discussing me as if I'm a peculiarly twisted stick lying on the ground.

In the mornings, I watch the vegetable garden several stories below my window, inside a wall. In winter the ground groans, but in spring it weeps green sprouts, and it's soothing to watch the bent backs of patients moving among the plants. Was that how those massas and missuses calmed themselves, eased their mortal fears? Watching the bent bodies and the sweat endlessly staining the ground, mojoed by sorrow voices?

At night, when the chatter from the other patients fades into whispery sighs and moans, I stretch myself full out on the bed and listen to the sound of old water falling on rusty metal.

Plink, plink. Water dripping from who knows. At sunrise, I often glimpse a sparkle in the corner of my eye. But from somewhere beyond the barred windows it falls, and I can't waste the energy to look out and see where it comes from.

So there in the dark or sometimes in a night awash with moonlight, I wander through memory and the dripping is my companion. Sometimes it seems closer, right there in the room with me. It always seems closer on those nights when I'm on the ship and something, once again, is rubbing me raw. I don't even shout out the pain anymore. It's too familiar to fuss about. The dripping sound is very loud on those long nights, but in the morning there're only a few wet circles on the floor—blood, not water. And no one says anything about the red stains in the bed.

Only the next day, Dr. Carl Cremrick, assigned to my case, will begin by asking, "How have your dreams been lately, Elizabeth?" And I will begin and end with silence.

Dr. Cremrick and I spend those daily sessions staring at each other while he talks and asks and sometimes stares at the barred windows. Some days his white self is as pink as a newborn pig. His bald head glows. Other times he's washed out and pale and sad-eyed. I know he dreads seeing me. I feel his dread moving in front of him as he makes his way down the hall to my room.

But he comes every day and he always takes notes. Who knows. Maybe it's his to-do list.

The halls are quiet for once. My door stands open these days—"I think the real danger is past," I hear Cremrick tell one of the nurses. "She seems calm. As a matter of fact, she's been calm from the beginning. No sign of any disturbances that even hint at the violence she does to herself. Frankly, I haven't even figured out how she does it. Have you been searching her things?"

"Yes," the nurse says. "Maybe she's got a piece of glass somewhere."

"More than likely she's just been reopening the stitches with her fingernails. Please tell the nursing assistant to cut them again. We might have to try something else. In any case, keeping her in her room has been no good. So let her mingle, but keep an eye out, and I don't have to tell you to call at the first sign of anything. And when you see her, take note of those scars. See if there's any fresh wound."

So the door is now ajar. I wear the jeans that I so painstakingly embroidered a year or so ago. I'm going out of my room alone for the first time since I got here six months ago.

Someone sings a thin tone. Well, more like a humming whine, coming from two or three rooms down the hall.

"Shut up," comes another voice. "Shut up, if you can't sing that song right, just don't sing it!"

I stand in the doorway. Not a soul is in the hall; I'm alone except for the singing voice. The passage stretches so far I can't see the end, just doors, some closed, some not.

The singing stops. But now there's music. Old songs from old souls, digging in deep to scoop out the pain.

I move down the hall, trying to step closer to the sound of the record crackling and popping on some turntable somewhere. I stumble a little and stop to lean against the wall. I can't hear anything but that song, a blues wail, and Grace slips close to me, prodding me to take another step. It's a step into the past.

The hall seems to go on forever and Grace's arms hurt from the weight of the suitcase. She dreads the thought of hauling up the trunk sitting on the living room carpet downstairs in the rooming house.

The singer presents her woe in a feminine growl. *See?* she sings. *See what you have done?* There are three doors in the hall. Two are closed and she stops at the open one, where the song greets her from a record player and the room's occupant, a woman, looks up as Grace puts down her suitcase, shaking the ache from her fingers.

"New, huh?" The woman seems about forty or so, with all kinds of hard edges. Her voice, her worker's hands, her mouth set in a thick line. She sits alone on the bed wearing a ripped cotton slip and a head full of pin curls. She waits for acknowledgment, never blinking.

"Which is number three?" Grace asks.

"Right next door to me. Only one empty now." The woman gets up to stop the record, spinning on a player in the corner. She turns it over. "I hope you don't mind the music. I gotta have my music."

"No, no," says Grace quickly. "It's real nice."

"From Bama, right?"

"How'd you know?"

"It's all over you. I used to walk like that, talk like that. Then it got too hard to be the woman my mama taught me to be, ya know?" She looks at Grace's tall, upright figure, swaying slightly in the doorway. Her worn-out, but mercilessly starched, cotton dress. The hat. The gloves. None of it new, but all of it good. "Yeah," the woman says. "I was from Alabama. But not no more."

Grace shifts nervously from one foot to the other, sorry now that she stopped. Shoulda just found the room and gone in. This woman looks like she wants to give Grace all her business and Grace certainly doesn't want it. She's in a new place a long way from home and not ready to get friendly with the neighbors. Already Detroit exerts its differences. Back home, she wouldn't have hesitated to engage a new acquaintance in a long, fruitful conversation.

But all the woman says is, "My name Tessie. You need help with your thangs?"

"No, Miz Parker's brother is bringing it up. I'm Grace Lancaster. Real nice to meet you."

Tessie just nods and gets up to look out the window, her back to the door. Grace takes this as a signal that the conversation is over and picks up her suitcase again.

She feels her feet there on the ragged carpet of Mrs. Parker's upstairs hall, yet the smell of the place is definitely antiseptic.

Grace has pulled me completely into this recollection and I adjust to the feeling of being two places at once. But almost as soon as I do, my vision clouds some. There's Tessie with her back to us, and we still hold the case lightly, but our hand no longer aches.

I'm crazy, I think. *I'm so crazy, I want to weep.*

We close our eyes and let go of the suitcase handle, expecting to hear a thud on the floor. But there is silence until a question intrudes.

"What in the world are you?" someone asks. Not Tessie, but someone standing less than five feet away and—down. It's a thin little voice, so quiet that it seems to be straining to hear itself.

I shake my head, trying to clear the fog that has descended, and I see that the woman standing there isn't a worn, mahogany-skinned creature with hard eyes. She's small and white—from the top-most hair on her head to the little satin mules on her feet. Gray eyes that look right through you. Behind her a record sobs on the turntable of a small stereo. Blues. Why is this Daughters of the Confederacy matron spinning that blues record?

I shiver and pull my sweater closer around my body. Surely

there must be someplace Daddy could have sent me where I wouldn't have had to endure so many white people. As crazy as this world has made us, surely there must be a place.

"I asked you, what are you?"

I should go, keep walking.

"Oh, a nontalker, eh?" She smiles, revealing a perfect set of obviously fake teeth. "I don't blame you. I don't blame you one bit. Best not to talk around here, they use it against you. But I saw you."

She steps into the doorway and peers around my body as if expecting to see someone else listening. Then she grabs my arm and pulls me in the room. I snatch my arm away, but I'm already inside. She shrugs, asking, "Do you want something, dear? I have Gatorade."

I just stare at her while she pours herself a glass of the light green liquid.

"Now," she says, after taking a sip and settling into an old easy chair near the window. "I won't tell anybody. And I ain't afraid. I've heard about these things." She leans forward, whispering, "But I did see you, you can't deny that. First you were there, then she was. You look kind of alike but she's a little taller. Darker. Wearing a hat and gloves and carrying a suitcase. Pretty nigger girl. I saw her. Smiling and talking. Couldn't hear what she was saying, but saw her clear as day."

This blows my mind, or what's left of it. She saw me. Us. Grace. I find myself wandering into the room a little further.

"It's OK, hon. I won't tell nobody." She gets up again and looks out the door. I wonder why she doesn't close it, since she's so concerned about people listening in. She comes back in and smiles at me. "Come by and see me any time you want. I

notice you listening to my record. I love those blues. I used to
know people who sang it for real. Not on a record. But I'll tell
you sometime. Come on back. And bring that other gal with
you."

"Elizabeth." The nurse, the short fat one, was in the doorway. "There you are. Having a visit, huh? That's great. Hello,
Mrs. Corday."

"Patsy, how are you?"

"Fine, fine. I'll be by later with your medication. It's almost
time. Meanwhile, maybe it's a good idea for Elizabeth to get
back to her room."

I'm already out in the hall, making my way back.

"Well, she's not bothering me," I hear Mrs. Corday say. "Not
a'tall. I like the quiet ones."

Cremrick comes with a large sketch pad and colored pencils.

"I thought," he says, placing the pad on my bed next to me,
"today we would try drawing something. I know that you
draw. Your mother told me."

I already feel my mind drifting. I stare down at the blue
house shoes I'm wearing—a birthday gift from my mother last
year. He puts the pencils on top of the pad and sits in the room's
only chair, a gray-metal thing with no padding.

"Nothing wrong with trying a different kind of communication," he says. "Pictures. And maybe you could have fun with
it as well."

I'm busy! I want to scream at him. *Don't you understand? I'm
busy, busy, busy. I've got things to remember. I ain't got time to draw
doodles for you.* I open my mouth to yell, but nothing comes out,
and I close it to merely stare, frowning, at his bent head.

I wonder if he knows he's the perfect neutral surface on which to superimpose my mental wanderings, explorations. If I were to talk, which I'm not inclined to do right then, I would tell him so just to annoy him.

"Your mother tells me you were quite imaginative as a little girl." He crosses his legs in that prissy way I hate for men to do. They stack their legs up and jiggle their foot and perhaps, as Cremrick just did now, they clasp their hands around the knee. So now he sits there like a knot, talking but not really looking at me. Looking somewhere right above my eyebrows.

"Yes," he continues. "She was quite enthusiastic about your drawing and painting. There's more than one way to talk, eh? And well, after all this time, Lizzie, you must have something to say. You must have something inside about to burst. Long time to walk around burdened." He leans over to pick up the pad and pencils. "How 'bout I start? I used to draw a little long time ago . . ."

I can't look at him. For a minute, I can't stand to be there. Usually it's fine, though I can't say that Bentwood is a spa or anything. But it's fine when they leave me alone to my thoughts, to my pasts.

Ayo is silent; she tries always to let things float on the air around her. Once she got whacked on the head because she refused to answer a question from the mistress. It was a personal question, and heaven knows, there wasn't nothing to own but your private loves and hates and white people wanted those too. They wanted to own the unknowable. So Ayo stayed silent and thought of ways to get through and live to tell.

Ayo paces back and forth inside my head. Restless and yearning, impatient for me to remember all. But Grace holds our secrets just beyond my view, eagerly teases me with imminent revelations. She's there now, insisting that I listen to her, insisting that I don't have to pay mind to a damn thing Cremrick says, which isn't much anyway.

I glance again at the doctor. He scratches away at the pad with a blue pencil, as quietly gleeful as a child, his gloom lifted for the moment. I want to laugh, because I approve of the color, a deep true blue.

Yes, we like blue, Grace says. *Night blue. Night coming on at sunset.*

I stare at the pad and his white fingers moving back and forth. There are stars underneath the pencil and clouds moving across the moon. The wind touches the trees briefly and I think I hear someone calling my name.

For a moment, I see only moon and sky. Then I look down at my hands. I wear a gold wedding band and the surface under my palms scrapes roughly against the skin. Wood. A porch railing.

OK. Gone again. I'm glad I can't hear Cremrick anymore.

"Grace! Where you at, girl?"

"Here on the porch, George, you ain't gotta yell."

Grace hears heavy steps on porch boards. She doesn't hear the door open, but firelight makes the leap from the inside onto the wood and across the spare steps that lead down to the yard. He comes to stand beside her, the only man in Johnson Creek taller than she is. Grace wonders if that's why she married him. But when he reaches up and gently rubs a callused hand across the back of her neck, she remembers that isn't the only reason.

"You tired, huh? Me too," he says. "But tomorrow's Sunday."

"What you think on the other side, George?"

"The other side of what?"

"That." Grace points up over the pine trees. "The sky. We stand here and all we see is Johnson Creek, but all them other places are in the same time as us, right? We forget, 'cause we can't see 'em. We can only see here."

"So?" He laughs and slips his hand down and around Grace's waist, hugging her to him. "I guess I don't want to be no other place. Hell, girl, I just got married! That all I got on my mind."

"You ole thang!" She jabs him playfully in the ribs.

"Oh, yeah. Old. nineteen or so. I got a few on you. But you talk like an old person sometimes, Grace." He draws back to look at her. "And sometimes . . . like now . . . asking thangs that children do. Where do the stars come from, and all that."

"Don't you just ever want to go someplace else, George? Someplace new?"

"Well, I guess I ain't too comfortable with new thangs, you know. People leaving, though. Jesse told me today he's leaving. That old buzzard Gelks don't want to never let him off that land, and well, I can't blame Jesse much, but I miss him already. You know, Grace, we's lucky to have this little bit of ground to stand on, on our own two feet. You ma was sho' generous about it. Yes, Joy a smart woman."

"She got that from my grandmother, she says." Grace glances over her shoulder to where a pinpoint of light burned in the window of her mama's small house. "You know she and old Bessie bought it long time ago. Not much. But ours. I swear, I used to think this little piece of land was the only thing that kept me here."

"I hear that's changed," George says teasingly. "I hear there are other thangs keepin ya now."

"Yeah, I been ruint. Ruint by some tall man."

"Quite a fella, huh?"

"Ummmm . . ."

"Hey!" He laughs and shakes her in mock anger and Grace trembles with joy and that other thing that is still so new.

He puts his hand on my shoulder and shakes again gently, and the stars fade and thin light come through barred windows.

Cremrick clutches a fistful of my white shirt.

"OK, Lizzie. Don't leave me, now. If you don't want to participate, that's fine. We can come back to it."

I blink. Grace. There was Ayo first, then Grace. Two of them. They both mention Joy, but I have none of her memories.

Cremrick tucks the pad under an arm with an annoyed gesture. He says something, but I don't hear him.

December 1995 — Tuskegee

The pictures I've designed for that quilt so obviously tell Grace's story that I'm beginning to think Mother is deliberately pretending to be the densest woman on the planet.

It's too cold now to work in the attic, so she has relented and permitted the quilt pieces to stay on the dining room table between meals. Almost daily now, we sit there sewing. We lay the blocks out in order as we finish them. Some days before I get to the table, she has taken them out already and arranged them and I often come upon her standing there, looking down, transfixed for a few long seconds, before she realizes I'm there.

She's there on Christmas Eve, standing in the little bit of sunlight that ventures through the windows, her hair messy, escaped from the ball at the back of her neck. It forms a little-girl halo around her face, which is half-turned away from me. She's been bustling around all day, cooking and putting up the last few decorations before our relatives invade tomorrow.

She looks up as I come in.

"You know my mother was an artist," she says quietly. "She could make the most wondrous things out of scraps of cloth that I didn't think were good for nothing."

I sit down at the table and begin threading a needle, sensing that this is not the time to speak.

"I always wanted to be an artist like she was," Mother says. "I always wanted to be that tall, graceful beauty that she was. She was well named." She looks at me, smiling. "You remind me so much of her. Or what I remember of her, which isn't much, I guess."

"You never used to talk about her when I was little, Mother," I say.

"It wasn't because I didn't . . . think about her." She sits at the table.

"She left you," I say bluntly, steeling myself against the sharp pain that needles its way through my chest and throat.

"And I never found out why." She stares at the quilt pieces almost hungrily. I wonder if this is the moment; I want to twist in my seat, but I will myself to be still.

"I think Aunt Eva knows," she says. "I think she and Mary Nell knew." She gets up and walks around the table.

"There is a way to know," I say, quietly.

"What?" She paces in a small circle.

"Ask me anything you want to know." I put down the needle and the fabric.

"Oh . . . oh." Mother puts a hand to her throat, as if she's choking. "I should not be discussing this with you. Of all people. After what you went through . . ."

"I'm probably the one person in the world you can talk to about Grace," I say, leaning towards her.

"Baby, I don't know. I'm sorry I brought any of it up. I mean, you used to think you were her," she says, orbiting the dining room table. "I couldn't stand it if you . . . falling back into that . . ." She pauses. " . . . that state of mind."

"I'm not. Mother, I'm never going back to that. Never."

"But you ARE!" she yells. Her voice has been rising and now she's yelling. "I thought you were over that. I thought you were OK!"

"Mother . . ." I stand up and go to her, touching her arm. She stares down again at the fabric, a sob slipping through her lips. I've been working on the last block; they're almost ready to sew together. "Mother . . . I'm fine. Nothing's going to happen."

"It's my fault, isn't it?" she whispers. "Are you going to be sick again?"

"I was never sick, Mother. Just lost."

"Lost?"

"Lost. And I'm not going to go there again."

"It's my fault," she whispers again. She picks up a quilt block and then drops it as if the fabric is on fire. She backs out of the room before turning to escape.

October 3, 1899

Ole Miz Ward the one Mama say that put dem marks on her back in the first place. Yep she meaner than hell till the day she die. Even as a young woman she was. Her husband bought me for a lady maid for her.

She jest married then. 17 years old and lordin it over the whole house.
Two houses I should say. One in town and another bigger one between
here and Smuteye. They was rich even by white folks reckonin. When I
came there I still couldnt understand nobody really. And they set me up
with another maid and the cook Mary to teach me to speak and act
right. But lordy I didnt know what they was talkin about. I was scairt
all the time. Mary was scairt so I was too. I didnt know till later that
she was scairt for me cause I werent learnin nothin. They had that big
ole house you know the one and I was supposed to run around all day
fetchin and fannin and bowin to Miz Ward. But I didnt understand
what she was askin me to do so she would say somethin and I would just
stand there and watch her face turn purple. I never got tired of watchin
her face turn different colors. That was new to me. So one day Im
walkin in the backyard carryin water from the pump and Miz Ward
lean out a window upstairs and screams somethin. So I just stop in my
tracks. She screams again but I dont understand so I just keep walkin
to the back door with the water and put it in the kitchen. Im on my way
back to the pump when she comes flying out of the back door screamin
at the top of her lungs. She carryin one of them parasol things and she
dressed real fine in pink silk and lace from head to toe. I stop and look
at her scairt but not knowin what to do. Mary runs out of the house
and stands in front of me but the missus just hits her with the parasol
and Mary hits the ground. Then she swat at me but she miss me and
then she run round the side of the house like a jackrabbit that big dress
bobbin. I done put the bucket down and tryin to help Mary get up when
she comes back with two men. Big muscular hands. And Im scairt but
Ida been even more if Ida known what she was up to. Shes carryin a
whip and them two mens hold my arms while she whip me cross the
back. Oh daughter she was laughin while she done it and them mens
wouldn't look at me while I buck and try to get away. My dress fell away
in big pieces and the blood ran down in the dirt and her pink dress was
all splattered. Mary whimpered over the water pump and Im sure my

hollerin could be heard from here all the way to Afraca. I looked up into one of them mens face and his grip slipped or maybe he let it slip and I ran I ran until I fell in the chicken yard with my face in the dirt and laid there for what seem like a long time. Den them same mens came and lifted me up so gentle and took me away. I wanted so much to die. I try to make it happen. I ask the spirits to take me. But they wouldnt even let me black out. They took me way from the house. We was almost to the door of Marys cabin when I heard the carriage leaving and I turned my head and saw Miz Ward sittin up there. She had changed her dress. Now she had on baby blue.

April 1981 — Montgomery

They put me in the garden and give me a spoon to dig up weeds. Several of the other patients from my floor are out there that day, including Mrs. Corday, who hums "St. Louis Blues" a couple of rows away.

At first I won't go. The male attendant pushes the spoon into my numb fingers. I wince as he spins me around—by the shoulders—and points to the garden, saying very loudly, "I know you understand me. We're working in the garden today. You can start anywhere, just get the weeds out."

I try to block out the throbbing pain in my back and the sudden fear crowding my brain and take a slow walk towards the rows of sweet potato plants. A glance over my shoulder tells me that Cremrick watches from the porch.

By the time I make it there, I'm inside the fear, looking out. It surrounds me like a cage. Can I refuse? What will happen to me if I do? The rows stretch forever; the modest garden becomes endless.

"Don't be scared, girl," says Mrs. Corday, who has stepped over several rows to stand behind me. "Just pretend like you working. They have gardeners. This is just to keep us busy."

I can't.

"I wish I knew how you do that," she says cheerfully. "Change like that. Why, you can't be no more than thirteen. One day you're a woman, today you're a girl. And a dark little thing at that. I've never seen a colored girl as colored as you."

Ayo is here. She is the terror that renders me motionless. She stands in the field with her hoe, wondering where to go, but knowing there is nowhere. She stands there as her lifetime of work begins, surrounded by others bending and straightening up and down as far as her eyes can see.

Now would be a good time to speak, to break through the bubble I'm looking through, the one that holds all of time in this one moment. But I can't. Her silence belongs to me, just as every other part of her life belongs to me. Her pain, her fear and her blood, the stuff running down my back and legs and into the rich Alabama dirt.

Mrs. Corday stares at me in awe and then begins to fuss over me, wiping at the blood with the hem of her dress. "Can you teach me how to do that?" she whispers.

After that, they give me a shot four times a day and a nurse sits in my room all night every night for two weeks. It's a good time for dreaming.

Once, I wake and the nurse is standing over me anxiously.

Mistress Ward in her pink antebellum dress has been parading around in my dreams, and the sheets are stained. The nurse looks into my eyes and then to my wrists. I smile; I know she's been watching the blood ooze from my body and been too paralyzed, too fascinated to do anything. She opens a bag she has with her, and bandages me without speaking.

"It's been what, seven months, Elizabeth?" Daddy walks the room diagonally and I follow him with my eyes. "Your mother can't stand to come right now, but I have to. You're the same every time I see you. Silent. Bandaged up." He takes a deep breath. "They said don't be negative. Although," and he talks a little louder now, looking at me, "it's obvious they don't know what they're doing. The only thing that's keeping me from moving you is that every psychiatrist I've talked to says moving you might be worse for you than this." He goes to the barred window and looks out. "What could be worse than this I don't know."

I know I'm dreaming. 'Cause I always know now.

The full-brown woman walks through the dream and asks if I know her. Of course, I say. I sit cross-legged on my hospital bed, but it's outside in the middle of the garden, not among the sweet potatoes, but in the flower plots beside the sunflowers. And someone hums a very old song, there behind the roses.

She sits beside the bed, in the dirt, her beautiful blue garment a swirl around her elegant body; she seems to rise from a slightly restless sea. She takes my hand.

This is the hand of my mother, she says. *And of my grandmother. Petals of the flower. Your life is many lives.*

I lie down on the bed among the blooms and wake up surrounded by my room.

A few days pass before Cremrick and the others notice that
the scars have healed. They leave ugly marks that I will carry
with me forever, but the grim wounds have closed over.

"Those scars look . . ." He looks at me probingly. "They look
a few years old, I'd say. Now I know you were bleeding down
there in the garden just a week ago. What is going on with you,
Elizabeth?"

Of course, I don't answer. I don't even think he expects it
anymore. He just shakes his head and makes notes.

"I think I'll change your medication," he says.

I'm only getting two shots a day now.

May 1996 — Johnson Creek

Anthony Paul. Anthony Paul. Anthony Paul.

I lie on the warm grass in Eva's backyard, right at the edge of her sprouting cornfield, kinda whispering his name in my head. I hear his voice, cool and deep like an underground river, wandering out of the windows of the house, where Eva bribes him with biscuits and last year's dewberry jelly.

We laughed all the way down the road from Tuskegee. Son Jackson greeted us from his porch as we drove up. I bounded up Eva's front steps and followed my nose into her kitchen, where she had a midday meal cooking.

"Expecting company?" I asked, crinkling my nostrils at the scent of baking biscuits and lifting the lid on a bubbling pot of turnip greens.

"Just you—and him," she answered, nodding towards An-

thony Paul, whose lanky body had just appeared in the doorway.

"Stop that clairvoyant stuff, Eva," I said, smiling. "It's
spooky."

"*I'm* spooky?" she whispered, sniffing and then turning to
Anthony to hold out her hand and smile.

Now they're buddies, and I stretch out there trying to decide
whether to introduce a serious subject on such a bright day. I
had thought to bring him here, to the house in the woods. A
test, I suppose. But also I need to tell him some things.

He comes out onto the back porch, rubbing his stomach. He
looks startled when I emerge from the corn, but lets me take his
hand.

"Where are you taking me?" he says, laughing. I just smile
and keep walking until we come to the bridge. I sit with my feet
over the edge, watching the water tumble underneath us. We
can see the top of Eva's house in the distance. Grace's world lies
beyond the trees.

He sits next to me and I weave his fingers through mine.

"What is it?" he asks.

"Anthony . . . " I start but can't arrange the words so they'll
come out right.

"I'm not going to freak," he says, letting go of my hand and
slipping his arm around me. "Whatever it is." Still I don't
speak. "Are you going to tell me?" He asks. "You know, you're
scaring me a little."

"That's OK," I say, looking long at him, then getting to my
feet and holding out my hands. "Because it's really scary. Come
with me."

He doesn't ask any more questions, but walks with me into

the trees, into the past, where Grace's tired old house stands, sagging even more than last time I saw it, but still there.

I lean on what's left of the fence that used to lie between the house and their pasture. Anthony Paul touches my shoulder.

"Are we going in there?" he asks.

"I don't know." I shake my head. "The last time I was here . . ."

He waits.

"The last time I was here," I begin again, "I went back in time."

Anthony Paul is quiet for a minute and then goes up to the house to look into one of the windows.

"Whose house is it? Who lived here?" he wants to know.

"I did. Back in the thirties."

He turns slowly around to face me, frowning.

"This house originally belonged to my great-great-grandmother. She was a freed slave. Back then it only had two rooms."

"But you said you . . ."

He stops speaking when I go over to him and gently press my palm to his lips.

"Later on my grandmother Grace lived here with her husband George. He added another room." I sigh, going to the window and leaning into the old bedroom.

"The last time I was here," I continue, "I sat right on that floor in there and closed my eyes. And when I opened them, I was back there, with Grace and George. I was living her life. Just for a while. But I was there."

"What do you mean you were there?"

"Look. Ever since I was fourteen, I've been having these . . .

visions. At least that's the only word that comes close to what happened to me. Not only do I remember Grace's life, I remember Bessie's, the slave's. And her name really isn't Bessie. It's Ayo."

"Does this have something to do with the scars?"

I nod. "I used to be able to actually feel Ayo's pain. I used to bleed like she did, in the same places she did."

Anthony Paul's gaze falls to the scars on my wrists.

"When I was about twenty, once I woke up with my body on fire and covered with blood. I can't even describe the pain. The next day I was admitted to my first mental hospital. Everyone thought I was trying to kill myself."

"Were you?"

"No! I had no control over what was happening. I didn't know what was happening at first. But I sorted it out."

"What did you come up with?"

"Well." I brace myself for his incredulity. "Reincarnation."

"Reincarnation?"

"Yes. You see, I think that Ayo reincarnated as Grace and Grace reincarnated as me. Grace had to leave her home and her family because Ayo's memories became too much for her to handle."

He moves a little away from me. Sighing, I wonder if my terror tale of blood and wandering souls has lost him to me forever. I rest my back against the house's tired old boards. I can almost feel it sinking into the earth.

"So that's why you were in the hospital. A suicide attempt."

"No. Are you listening? I didn't, I wouldn't do that. The wounds just came."

"Lizzie, I'm sorry. I mean . . ." He sighs, looking back at the house. "I think your father was wrong to do what he did—put you away like that. God—fourteen years. But what you're telling me, I don't know. Reincarnation?" He shakes his head.

"I'll be honest," I say, walking up to him and cradling his face in my hands, forcing him to look at me. "I'm taking a chance by telling you this. The doctor—my father—is still legally my guardian. You could go tell what I told you—that I still believe that I'm Ayo, that I still believe that I'm Grace—and that would be the end of me. I'd probably never see the outside again. I'm trusting you with my life. I don't blame my father, really. He just doesn't know. But . . . if he thought I was sick, he'd feel like he had to do something about it. Just like last time."

"Lizzie." He covers my hands with his and slides them down to my wrists, gently caressing the scars. "I would never—never—do anything to put you back there. I can't even stand the thought that you were there in the first place." He closes his eyes against the moisture that I see just beginning to glisten on his lower lashes. "I'm not letting you go back."

I touch the little tear at the corner of his eye, then lean forward to kiss his lips very softly. He lets me walk into his arms and I put my forehead on his chest, relieved at least that he's still here.

"I know it's hard to believe," I whisper. "But I know, I *know*, who I am. And *you* know who I am."

"What . . . ?" He steps back, but not far, still encircling me in a loose embrace.

"See . . . that painting of yours, the one you said is me."

"Yes . . . ?"

"It's a picture of Ayo. It's me, but it's Ayo. You see?" I lift my arms and hold them out. "These scars, the ones that bled, are the marks of that woman."

"Wait a minute. I don't know . . ." He breathes a little fast now, his grip tightening on my arms.

"I know you've thought about this. We've met before," I say quietly, simply, holding his gaze. "I don't know where, I don't know how. When. We might not ever figure that out."

"Lizzie . . ."

"You never ever asked me about the scars. Not even the ones on my back. I know how bad they are. You didn't even seem surprised by them."

He shakes his head and looks at the ground.

"Are you sure? I mean . . . oh, shit, this is too deep."

"No. It's simple. It really is." I slip my arms around him, trying to make contact with as much of him as possible. This would be more than I had hoped for, to have this gift, this other soul to continue with on the journey. It would be such magic if he took the next step to me. I undo two buttons on his shirt, burrowing my hands inside to lay them right up against his chest. His heart pounds.

"Anthony Paul, do you love me?"

"Yes," he whispers. A child's whisper.

"Then that's all I need right now, I guess. But this ain't going nowhere. It ain't the beginning or the end. Someday you'll believe that."

The soft fall of cloth wakes me later that night. He stands beside the painting, touching her face with his fingers.

His silence now is merely an extension of the long quiet that rode with us back to Tuskegee. Afterwards, he said little, just undressed me slowly and drew me to him on the bed, falling asleep with his face pressed between my shoulder blades.

"Anthony?" I sit up now, watching him standing there naked beside the canvas.

"I had a dream," he says quietly, turning to climb back in bed and embrace me again.

"Bad?"

"Yes." He squeezes me closer and is quiet.

October 18, 1899

Mary healed me up Mama say. I was two three weeks in her cabin flat on my stomach. That first day I just cry while she soak that blood up and spread salve on it. Something she made herself. She left in the morning and evening to go cook and I lay there by myself watchin the shadows made by the fire leapin at me. I would ask the spirits to take me home and then Id close my eyes thinkin they had come. But I always wake up in the same place. I was just blackin out most of the time. White man came next day a doctor I reckon and he look at me from the door. Never came near. Then he say somethin to Mary and left. You know daughter I think it was about then that I just went plum crazy. I needed to die and God wouldnt let me. I needed it so bad. I could taste death in the back of my throat and I had no need fo food. Mary fretted that she could not get me to eat nothin.

Long bout the fourth or fifth day I reckon I was jest lying ther on my belly, grindin my teeth fo the pain and feeling dizzy. It was morning and Mary was at the house. And the quilt at the door moved. We didn have no door just quilt or cloth or somethin. But anyways it moved aside and a woman came in. I didnt know her at first. My eyes was fogged up. Couldnt see straight atall. And the woman came in and stood by the bed. I didnt look up, I didnt move I hurt so bad but she kneel by the bed and look right in my face and daughter I swear it was my mama! Maybe I was dreamin or jest out of my head but I swear my mama was squattin right there all dressed in her Afraca clothes jest like I remember her. And she smile and I forget the pain for a while and went to sleep. I woke up a couple of times during the morning, and she still be there sittin on the dirt floor by the bed. Then I woke up cause Mary was coming in with dinner and Mama was gone. I began to cry and tried to tell Mary, but she still didnt understand me atall. But all during that night, I could feel her there. I didnt see her no more. But she was there with me. And the next day when Mary gave me food I ate it all.

After I was well, they puts me in the fields not long after that. I never saw the inside of that big house again and that suited me fine.

I July 1982 — Montgomery

sit in the gray metal chair dressed in flannel PJs, because, though it's summer, the AC makes me shiver. Time
for a session. The dripping sound echoes in my head. I
move the chair closer to the window and the sound becomes clearer.

I slide the window open and with my hand around the bars,
look out and up.

A drop of water falls, glimmering as it comes. It rushes past
my window to end with a familiar plink on some ledge below.
Almost immediately, I'm aware of another drop coming.

Just as I angle myself to try and see its point of origin, it starts
to rain. One of those little summer showers. The falling water
and the falling rain dance together. The sunlight still illumi-

nates the morning and the light transforms water droplets into jeweled links, turning and twisting beside the window.

Longtime Bentwood resident Mr. Johnny dances down in the garden below among the okra bushes, his sneakered feet flinging new-made mud.

He should be careful, Grace says. *That mud will never come out.*

Not today, I say. I'm tired.

It was raining that day.

I don't remember, I say, leaving the window. I go over to the bed and crawl under the covers, trying to concentrate on the sound of the water instead of my grandmother's voice in my head.

I got mud on my shoes and stockings. It never came out.

I don't remember. Leave me alone now.

You're never alone. Ayo has seen to it.

The rain whispers Ayo's name and Grace answers.

Grace talks to herself, alone in that bare Detroit rooming-house room. *Maybe she's gone,* she thinks as she folds the last bit of washing and puts it in her trunk. The room has no chest of drawers, no wardrobe. Just a bed and a table and a chair. She keeps everything in her trunk, even the permanently mud-stained stockings that she's spent most of yesterday trying to clean.

"Alabama mud," she says aloud. "Ain't nothing like it."

And it's still raining. All the way from Alabama to Detroit it rained and two days later, it continues to come down, coloring the pitiful cluster of buildings outside her window the same dirty gray. But despite all that, Grace sees the gleam of something that feels like hope. Because there are no visions. No voices. Not since she'd stepped on that train.

Maybe she's gone, she thinks again, sighing.

She puts the stained stockings in the trunk and closes the lid. *That's one thing I ain't gon' miss*, she thinks, *that mud, sticking to everything, looking like old, faded blood. People gon' think I got bleedin' feet.*

Grace laughs to herself, reaching down to take off the clean white stockings she wears. They are damp. The puddles on the streets of Detroit are as deep as ponds, and she's stepped in every one today, walking around looking for work. She pulls off one stocking and then the other, wondering at their sticky wetness.

"What is that?" she says out loud, looking down, and nearly falling out of the chair when she sees the blood oozing from her ankles.

"No." She stands up and begins to turn around and around in the small room. "No! I didn't leave my home and my husband and . . . " She breaks off on a sob. "My children for this. You supposed to be gone. Gone! Left back there in Alabama. Hoverin' round your grave or something. Not here! How far I got to go?"

There is no answer and Grace makes a feathery trail of blood on the floor as she walks back and forth, confined by the small space. She closes her eyes and then opens them, but the blood is still there, a red ring around her bare ankle. She suddenly feels too weak to stand and sits down hard on the bare wood, hearing the sound of metal clinking. The rain comes down on the deck, whipped into razor sharpness by the wind, and there is her blood still seeping from under the leg irons and washing away.

Grace whimpers. "Not here. I can't go here no more. Please." She lies down, pressing her body to the ship's deck, trying to stop it from rolling. "I'm tired, Ayo," she says. "I'm tired."

Then it is quiet except for the rain. She slowly raises her eyes and finds that the small room is once again around her, and she cries bitterly. This is all she has now, this room and Ayo's memories.

The knocking gets my attention. I'm sprawled on the floor, the tile cool under my cheek. I'm strangely comfortable there, but when I look up, Cremrick's face is peering through the small square window in the door and his key is already turning in the lock. He comes in and walks past me to close the window.

"Nasty out," he says, his thin lips crinkling. I sit up.

"The floor is not a good spot," he says, taking the chair. I get slowly to my feet and sit on the bed, examining my ankles. The scars haven't changed.

Cremrick talks, rambling, fingering a vase of roses beside my bed. My mother's. Thorns removed.

He drones on about his own garden. I hear the water falling.

"How does she get those roses so big?" he asks, to himself really. As far as he's concerned, I'm a mental vegetable.

"Manure," I say, watching the rain.

Just the right word to break a two-year silence, especially when you live on the funny farm.

Ruth and I are in the garden sitting among the groping ten-drils of purple-hull pea plants. My hand sifts the soil. I'm sup-posed to be weeding, but I am talking and Ruth is staring at me like I'm an alien being.

She's been in Atlanta, at college, and this is her first visit here. I am gently chastising her for not coming sooner.

"Mother told you, I guess. I understand why you didn't come before. There's not much to say to someone who doesn't talk back," I say, trying to sound sarcastic and a little pitiful at the same time. I'm not above fishing for sympathy.

"No," she agrees, not looking at me, but at the industrial gray main building.

I decide that I don't like Ruth's obvious discomfort. I'm not even sure I like her anymore. Can't expect her to be chatting it up the way she used to, I suppose. We're at a mental hospital. But still there's something about her that's gone. Something missing.

She smooths her super-straight hair—over and over—with long, red-tipped fingers. It's shoulder-length, a rich brown with glints of red, very complementary to her impeccable makeup. She looks like a beauty queen.

"You look like a beauty queen," I say.

"Well, I guess I am in a way," she smiles, for the first time since she'd been there. "I was Miss Sophomore last year. You still talk the same, not much different. Two years in a nut-house—not talking—after a suicide attempt. Well . . ." She looks away to where, a few rows over, Mr. Johnny dis-cusses global affairs with a tomato plant. "I guess I expected a new you."

I laugh quite loudly, distracting Mr. Johnny enough so that he stops talking momentarily, but then returns to his never-ending speech. I dust dirt off my palms. "It's a new me. Old, but new. I'll tell you a secret, Ruth," I say, dropping my voice conspiratorially. "I'm not crazy."

She gives me an uncertain look. Doesn't know if I'm kidding or kooky. Neither did I, though. "Isn't that what they all say?" she asks.

I laugh again.

"Strange," she says, almost to herself. "I guess I thought you'd lose your sense of humor."

"You've been watching too many bad movies, Ruth," I say, rolling my eyes.

"But two years . . ."

"I just needed to be quiet."

"Why? Why didn't you say something? Maybe you could have been out of here by now." She glances again at the building and I think I see her shudder slightly.

"It wouldn't have been that easy, I don't think. But also . . . how do I explain? Talking just took too much energy. The pictures, the memories that came into my head. Damn, Ruth. I can't even describe some of it."

"And then you just decided that quiet time was over?"

"Yeah."

"Do you practice in front of a mirror? Normalness, I mean?"

"No. Do you think I need to?"

She laughs and I'm wary. Maybe she's laughing at me. "You know I have no talent for tact," she says.

"I don't know. Maybe I don't know you anymore. You

seem . . . harder. I guess that'll help you be a good journalist, huh?"

Ruth frowns. "And what are you going to do, Lizzie?"

She has to ask. "Oh, umm." I dig my bitten-off fingernails into the ground. "If present trends continue, I'll probably spend the next twenty years trying to figure out what sanity is, and I probably won't." I look at her and she's closed her eyes and screwed up her face—like her head hurts.

"Sanity," she says to the ground, "is a mutual agreement between folks trying to control their world."

"Yeah?"

"Yeah. Men used to lock women up in asylums because the woman wanted to wear trousers or because they decided they didn't want to be good Christian matrons anymore. The definitions of sanity change every day."

"You know I didn't try to kill myself, you know that's not what happened at all."

She's quiet, but she opens her eyes and gives me a shuttered look. We used to be best friends and I want to be again. I look into her eyes again and the shutters open for a moment and I know she's thinking of the night at the creek—was it really only two years ago?—and she remembers how everything was, how everything is, with me. But something has made her afraid of it. Afraid of her own strangeness.

"I didn't attempt suicide, Ruth," I say. "I was hurt. You believe me, right?"

She reaches out and takes my hands in hers and, as always, I feel that heat that she radiates. Relief makes me sit up a little straighter. At least that hasn't changed. She turns my hands over, sliding her fingers over the scars on my wrists. At first it's an examination, then a communication between us. Her hands are very warm. A spasm of pain crosses her face, then it's calm again.

"I'm sorry they hurt you," she whispers, with a secretive, painful smile. She's crying a little. "I don't know why they have to do that."

"So I won't forget again."

June 1996 — Tuskegee

In the quiet I hear a woman humming. For a few moments, I continue what I'm doing—melding the quilt layers together with small, straight stitches. With the return of warm weather, the project has ascended once again to the attic. I've shown Mother how to quilt, how to make the pictures we've sewn down move in whatever direction our needles decide and I watch with what can only be described as growing pride at her enthusiasm.

After a while, I figure out that I'm the one droning that little tune. Happy. That's what it is. The last time I truly felt that emotion I was a child. So now I'm starting over. Again.

"Elizabeth!" Daddy's quiet roar precedes him. "Are you up here?"

"Yeah, Daddy."

He awkwardly hauls a long cardboard box up the attic stairs.

"What's that?" I put down my sewing.

"Surprise. Where's your mother?"

"She's at Uncle Phillip's . . . he's not feeling well and she took him some dinner. She should be back by now. Daddy." I start to smile. "What is it?"

"Well," he says, almost shyly, "I saw as how you and your mother were working so hard . . . I figured I'd help things along, you know. The lady at the store told me that this was an all-around frame, sturdy and everything . . ." He's lifting something out of the box and I stare at a large wooden quilt frame, which he starts to set up in the middle of the floor.

"Daddy . . . it's great." I get up to hug him.

"I just wanted to make my own contribution to the project," he says. "I've just got to tighten a few things first, before you use this. Don't want anything to fall down." He has his screwdriver out.

"Well, this is good," I say. "Now we'll be able to do it up right."

He smiles slightly and works on the frame. I take up the quilting again and he stops to watch for a moment.

"I'm not familiar with that kind of thing, I guess. But it is beautiful." His eyes trace the outline of the cloth pictures. "You haven't lost your artistic touch, Elizabeth."

"Thanks. But I had help, you know."

"Yes. It seems to be a good thing for the two of you." I wonder if I detect a wistful note in my father's voice. My father the doctor, wistful?! But then he has been mostly on the sidelines since I returned, watching me like a hawk but not really coming too close. His gift seems to be his way of finally getting in the game.

"Maybe you can make one for me," he says now.

"No," Sarah says from the doorway, the top step creaking under her foot. "No. This one is for Mama. The next, for Lizzie."

Daddy and I turn simultaneously, both surprised. I try to catch her eye and when I do, she is not quick enough to hide that small glimmer of acknowledgment.

This one is for Mama. She believes, Ruth had said, she just doesn't want to.

"Well, Mother," I say, "a lot of me is in this one."

"I know that," she answers softly. "But . . . I guess I can't wait to do another one. It's been fun, you know? Educational."

"I had no idea you both were so talented," my father says, smiling.

This seems like a good time, so I take a deep breath. "You might have to do the next one by yourself, Mother."

She stares at me.

"I . . . um . . . promised Ruth I would go up to Atlanta for a while, help her do some things with that homeless foundation of hers."

"But . . ." Sarah's carefully constructed nonchalant expression slowly crumples. She begins to breathe rather hard. "We just . . . we just got started with . . . everything . . ." Her child's eyes bore a hole right through me.

"Well, I'm not going to leave until I've shown you every-thing, but after that you can go on by yourself." I want to hide from her hurt expression. "I'm not leaving forever," I add softly.

"I can't think of you going away again. Not now," she bit out.

"Why not now?" I put the quilt down on the table and rise from the seat. I see that she's fighting with herself, trying not to look at me, really look me in the face. *I'm here,* I say silently to her, knowing I can't push this, especially in front of Daddy.

She stands there with her arms folded rigidly across her chest. My father, my poor clueless father, ventures into the tension with, "You sure you want to do that foundation thing, honey? Ruth seems to be pretty swamped. It's a lot of work. Besides, we're just getting going again. As a family, I mean."

"I'm fine, Daddy. I'm not going to have a relapse," I say, voicing what he's thinking, but not taking my eyes off my daughter/mother.

"That's not what I meant." He frowns. "I just . . . you haven't been home for so long. I don't want you to go."

"Yes," Mother whispers. Then she turns her voice up a notch. "I don't want you to go. Not now. I'm still learning how to quilt."

"It won't be for a while," I say, taking a few tentative steps towards her. "We have time for everything." I put a hand over one of her clenched ones. She lets go of a breath she's been holding forever and curls her fingers around mine. I think of the children I left behind so long ago. Then, the twins were at that age when they didn't want to be associated with their mother. But little Sarah had been my shadow.

"No one's implying that you can't take care of yourself," Daddy says. "Just let me worry, OK. It makes me think you still need me."

Now I'm the one who is surprised and I'm sure the way I spun around in place to face him made that obvious.

"I know it was hard for you," he says. "Well, maybe I don't

know what it was like. Sometimes I feel . . . a little unsettled about . . . everything." He bows his head, as if praying. "You were away so long. Maybe I could have done better."

"It wouldn't have made any difference, Daddy." I step up to him and lean my forehead against his shoulder. "It was time I needed all along. Just time. That's what you gave me."

"I don't know if I can let you go again," Sarah says. She takes up the quilt and smooths the wrinkles out of the cloth.

"Yes you can, Sarah." She doesn't blink when I say her first name. "You're stronger than you know."

December 24, 1899

Our first Christmas Eve here wasnt even like Christmas at all Mama say. But it was joyful all the same cause we werent livin with white folk no more. That dont mean we didnt have to see them sometime but what a different life daughter! To be here livin with the quiet trees. We didnt have nothin. Took everythin Sam had to buy land but he was one of the lucky ones. Lots of folks just stayed where they were kept livin in dem same ole shacks kept lookin at dem same ole white people every day of they lives. Some left. Soon as they heard the news they just dropped what they was doin and walk away. Dropped dem hoes and picks and left. Some folks ended up sharecroppin. But Sam and me—we was lucky. Or I should say, I was lucky to have him.

He bought this land from Johnson. Miz Ward she had to sell some of her land too but you know she werent never gonna sell to no niggers. She stood right there and looked in Sams face and said he stole that money. Now you didnt know your daddy. But he was a real fine man. Strong. He belong to a Mr. Redding who had a place near. Redding werent a very rich man not by white folk reckonin. He had Sam and four other slaves and him and his wife and children worked right there in the fields with the black folk. To get more money he hired Sam out

*to other folk as a carpenter. Your daddy was a real fine carpenter. Red-
ding let Sam keep some of the money. Not much but some. Your daddy
he wanted to buy us all. But dem Wards werent sellin.*

*Not long after freedom come he heard Johnson was sellin land to
anybody that had the means. He had come down far since the war. Was
tryin to hold on to that house his mama was so fond of. So he was sellin
some uncleared land he was desperate cause not a lot of white folks had
money at that time. So we got this. Nothin but woods that aint never
seen no ax. It was pretty but Sam worked like a mule to clear it and
try to make it somethin. I think thats what broke him. I think thats
what made Sam Jr. get up and go. I still have hope to hear from him
before I leave but I spect I wont. He alive. I would feel it if he was dead.
Sometimes I wish Ben had gone too. Better I never see him again than
he die like he did. Hes a restless spirit. And Im sure daughter that he
walks the earth again somewhere. I know, I know hes made his way back
to life.*

November 1986 — Birmingham

No bars here. The windows are wide and from the softly upholstered chair in my room, I imagine summer church suppers spread on the expanse of green grass that falls away down the hill away from the back of the clinic, where I, and my memories, now live. It's the kind of grass that stays green year-round, so that even now, in late fall, summer still has her foot in the door.

Funny how Birmingham looks an awful lot like Montgomery from here. But I have to admit that Smith-Rainey Residential Treatment Center is a better class of cage. No jail windows, just the glint of the high metal fence beyond the band of trees that ring the buildings. Still, it feels better.

The new blue sheets Mother bought are still in their plastic among the books and clothes and other things I seem to have accumulated in the years at Bentwood. I take the matching comforter out of its case and unfold it, wishing for Grace's quilt again to spread over my bed and become my island. I wonder where it is.

"She told me. She told me, and I wouldn't listen."

"Your mother?"

"Yes. I was always going off. She told me to stay close, while she worked, but . . . I don't know. I could smell something."

"A bad smell?"

"No, no. Something good. Food. I don't remember what, right now, but something was cooking."

"What was your mother doing?"

"She had her cloth spread out. Dark cloth, with many, many patterns. Her fingernails are blue."

"So . . . ?"

"My mother is talking with someone. Trying to make a bargain of some sort. First, I'm sitting there next to her and then I stand. She looks at me with a warning, but quickly goes back to her discussion."

"And that's when you wandered off?"

"Yes."

Dr. Brun, the psychiatrist, shifts in her seat and takes some notes. They all do that. They write and write and produce pregnant files about me that they just pass along to the next scribe after they tire of wrestling with my head.

This is where we left off last time. I can't help but think about how I want to be wearing some nice, fashionable clothes,

with my legs crossed, sitting there discussing some safer subject like being an only child or how I was secretly in love with
my father or anything else but this . . . again. And at the end
of the hour, I could grab my designer purse with the gold
clasp and sashay right out of here and downtown for cocktails
with an old college friend. Except I don't have any old college
friends.

I pluck some lint from the front of the faded blue shirt I wear.

"Elizabeth, I know you don't want to talk about this again.
But what's the point of being here if we don't get at the meaning of this . . . dream you keep having?"

"Dream, dream . . ." I push off from the floor with my feet
and tuck them under my thighs as the chair twirls round and
round on its swivel. Flying. "Not a dream, Doctor. Isn't this
where you came in?"

She won't answer. I watch her blur of a face passing on the
perimeter of the circle I make for myself. That was it, maybe. I
move and the world is still. I go so fast, through this life and the
next and the next, that they can't keep up with me. Of course
we are actors in many lives. Any other notion is obviously
ridiculous. She thinks that after all that pain and strain I just dis-
integrated. That that dust under Bessie Ward's stone marker in
Johnson Creek is all that's left of me.

But she doesn't know any better.

"I'm tired," I say to her, trying to slow down, then stop, the
swivel chair. "Let's stop."

"You're not doing yourself any good by avoiding talking
about it."

"Doctor," I say, leaning over her desk. "All I've done is talk about it for the past four years. I can't help it if you don't know the story yet."

"Elizabeth," she says, tapping her pencil on the stack of papers in front of her. "The story I heard was that you tried to kill yourself a couple of times—really bloody, I heard—that you sometimes couldn't discern what was real and what wasn't, that you refused to speak for two years. That's the story, isn't it?"

"You are so damned sarcastic. That's what I detest most about you so-called doctors. That smug sarcasm and those be-all, see-all, know-all smiles of yours." I keep my voice low, my own smile rigidly attached to my face. "You have no idea how complex the universe really is."

"Elizabeth." She sighs, swinging her chair to face the window. "I don't think I wanna know how complicated the universe is." She swivels back around. "Did you think that suicide would free you?"

"I never even considered suicide. Somebody lied to you."

"Why would they do that?"

"Things are not always what they seem, Doctor." I spin around in the chair once more. I surely want to get out.

I stop again, facing her, holding on to the edge of the chair seat. She shuffles the papers on her desk, pausing at a photograph, a closeup of my poor battered back. Then I smile a little, and I see a flicker of fear in her blue eyes. "You wanna see those scars, Doctor?" I ask, nodding toward the picture. "After you see them, you tell me if you think I did that to myself."

"That isn't necessary."

"You want to know, don't you?" I start unbuttoning my shirt.

"How are you going to make an educated diagnosis if you don't see it all?" I take my shirt off and let it drop. I'm not wearing a bra, so if anyone decides now is a good time to come in with a memo or something, they'll have a new piece of gossip. When I hold out my arms to her, over the desk, she leans back slightly, then recovers, dropping her gaze to my wrists. She looks for a long time and I turn them over so she could see that each wrist has a perfectly circular scar, raised above the surface of the skin on my arms.

Then, silently, I turn my back to her, satisfied with her short gasp.

Her gaze is hot, I can feel it as it steps tentatively through the maze of scars, from neck to waist and beyond, permanent remembrance of the power of time folded back upon itself. Proof of lives intersecting from past to present.

"Sad thing is," I say, picking up the shirt to slip it back on, "what you're looking at was rather commonplace back then. Scars like these. That's the thing, Doctor, I'm just a typical nineteenth-century nigger with an extraordinary gift. The gift of memory." I button the shirt without turning around. Her silence is heavy.

"That's all that sets me apart, really," I say, heading for the door. "I remember."

On Day 10 in the new and improved prison, Dr. Brun hands a book across the desk; blank pages stare back at me when I open it.

"I think a journal might be a useful tool for you," she says, in answer to my querying stare.

"What do you want me to do?" I ripple the sheets of paper, enjoying the sound, but not about to let her see anything akin to pleasure anywhere in the vicinity.

"You should document those dreams. It might help us."

"I don't need to write anything down. I'm not going to forget. Do you think I can forget my own life? Not now."

"Well," she says, gazing through the blinds and out to where the attendants rolled forgotten people up and down between the rose beds. It was outdoor time for the wheelchair crowd. "Well, you writing it down will help *me* get a handle on things, you know, help me keep track. Be as detailed as possible, please, Elizabeth."

"Preparing a paper, doctor?"

She laughs very loudly, startling me. She seems genuinely amused. "On you? Not yet. Maybe not ever. I'm not going to read the journal myself; you're going to read it to me. Only the parts you want to. It'll be completely private."

"If it were completely private, I wouldn't have to keep repeating the same memories to you over and over, would I?"

My parents come for Thanksgiving dinner. I tried to get home, but the doctor wouldn't approve it, the bitch. I remember she asked me, "If you've lived all these lives, why haven't you learned to be nice to people?"

"I tried nice. I was being nice back when I wasn't talking. No one wanted to hear how confused I was then. Kindness, you know, is useless with some folks and life really is short. Why waste your time?"

She thought I was being a smartass, so I didn't get to go home.

Mother is upset, imploring my father to take me out of the hospital.

"What kind of place is this, John, when they won't even approve of a holiday visit? They're not helping her and you don't have to do what they say. You can just take her out of here. You're her guardian." She cries into the cranberry sauce and the other patients look at her curiously. At the moment, she seems more lost than they do. I did this to her. First as her mother, then as her daughter. Always leaving her to cope with things she doesn't understand.

"Careful, Mother, they may want to sign you up," I say, not being sarcastic . . . really. Sometimes it's hard to believe she's my daughter; she can be so timid, almost. But I know her pain is my fault.

"Elizabeth, please," my father says warningly. "You're not helping."

"Hey, I'm mental, remember?" I stab my fork down hard on the plate, missing the slice of turkey. The noise startles my mother, who now dries her face with the napkin.

"Look, Mother, it's my fault, OK? I'm not getting along with the doctor. It's uncomfortable. I guess I made her mad. Don't worry about me."

"What else have I got to worry about?" she says.

It's a Wednesday. A week before Christmas. I'm going home this time. Made up with Dr. Brun. All you have to do is a little pretending and bam! A holiday pass.

The room is nearly empty, but a group in the corner talk to

the priest who comes around sometimes. Does his little charity work a couple days a week. I change the channel to *Jeopardy!* and sit on the best couch, reveling in doing what I want, just for a moment or two, before somebody comes in to treat me like the damn fool that they think I am.

"What is *To Kill a Mockingbird*," I murmur. The balding male contestant who rings in had drawn a blank. "*To Kill a Mockingbird. To Kill a Mockingbird!*" My voice echoes in the almost empty room and now I've drawn the attention of the group in the corner. That rude buzzer goes off on the show.

"Oh, sorry, Bill," says the host, shaking his perfect curls and smirking slightly. "The response is 'What is *To Kill a Mockingbird?*' "

"And people think I'm a moron," I say, apparently to myself, so I'm surprised to get a response.

"Why would anyone call you that?"

The priest stands at one end of the sofa. Looking around, I see his little group filing out. He has his coat over one arm.

"Ah, Father, I hope I didn't disturb you." Am I getting a Catholic-school flashback? He reminds me of Father Paul from Our Lady of Mercy. I wonder if Father Paul is still alive. I hope this guy isn't gonna preach; but then, he's Catholic. They don't do that. They discuss. That was always the funny thing about going to Catholic school in a Baptist town, especially if you weren't Catholic at all. Hail Marys by day and tent revivals by night.

"Nah, I was through," he says. He has the same premature gray hair Father Paul had. Gray eyes set in a pale but animated face. He's really short. "Father Tom Jay, from St. Joseph's. Just visiting."

"I could tell you were," I say, smiling. "I'm Elizabeth. Lizzie."

"You got a last name, Lizzie?"

"DuBose. Most of our charity visitors don't care what your whole name is."

He doesn't respond to this, just looks right into my face. Makes me uncomfortable. Most of them don't look you in the eye. They gaze at some point in the distance while demanding your most intimate musings.

"I guess you don't belong here, huh, Lizzie?" the priest says.

"That's what we all say in here, Father."

"You didn't say it, I did. But I'd bet money you don't belong here."

"Gambling, Father?" I feel a little smile tempting my lips and see amusement ripple under his skin and around the bones of his face.

"Yes, all that bingo has spoiled me, I guess."

I really laugh at this, a big laugh, entirely genuine. I haven't done that for a while and what he said wasn't even that funny. He smiles outright, then slips on his coat.

"I'll see you round, Lizzie."

"Father."

"Nah. Tom."

I watch him leave, thinking again that good old Father Paul must be dead by now.

" 'I don't think this journal will help,' " I read. " 'I don't know what the point is. The doctor still calls them mere dreams, but I know better.' "

Dr. Brun crosses her legs, but doesn't say anything. She sits in the chair; I'm on my bed. I continue.

" 'How can they be dreams when I remember them so clearly and so perfectly, vividly the same each time? They are memories, of course. What do I care if she doesn't care to know that?' "

"Elizabeth," Dr. Brun interrupts. "This journal is supposed to be a dream journal, not a critique of me. You're avoiding things."

"I'm not finished," I snap back. "And it's my fucking journal. I don't even have to read it to you if I don't want to." I slam the book shut.

There's a silence. Then she leaves her chair and sits in the chair beside mine, leaning forward. "You're right," she says, sighing. "I'm sorry, you're right. Do you want to stop?"

I glare at her and turn the page.

" 'That's how it is with all these doctors. You know, it's like someone boring a hole into you with their eyes.' " I glance up and that's exactly what she's doing, staring without blinking.

I stop and close the book and close my eyes.

"Is that it?" Dr. Brun says. "I was hoping you'd tell me more details about the dreams."

"No. I remember them fine," I say. "Some things aren't made to be forgotten. And it's not the memories that are important right now. It's how I feel about them."

"And how do you feel about them?" She touches my hand briefly and settles back in her chair to listen, her fingers making a little tent under her chin.

I am so damn tired of this.

"Let's get it over with; what's your story?"

The priest, Tom, startles me. Again. I'm finally sitting out on that green expanse of grass on a blanket, wrapped in a large sweater. It's cool, but the sun is fierce, as if it has decided December needs some new energy. I'm not even thinking to myself, so I'm certainly not prepared to hear somebody talking. But there he is. I'm not happy about that.

"Shouldn't you be with your group?" I ask, peering around him, hoping to see them trailing behind.

"My group?"

"Those people I saw you with last time."

"Oh, they were just some people I ran into. I don't have a group. I just come in and talk to anybody who wants to talk."

"Do you think I want to talk? You're not a head doctor, are you? Dr. Father? Father Ph.D.?"

"No." He laughs and to my annoyance folds his abbreviated body to sit next to me on the grass. Not, thank God, on my blanket. "I don't have the patience to stay in school that long. Not interested anyway."

I watch a group of patients sitting under a tree; they have three chess games going and from the frowns on their faces, the competition is heated. Of course, people frown all the time here.

"So," the priest begins again. "What's your story?"

Persistent devil. He must be getting my body language, but he makes no move to leave. And he's asking questions.

"I'm crazy, Father."

"I thought we'd already established that you don't belong here."

He says this quite casually, leaning back, his face turned towards the sky as if in supplication.

"Well, then, I'm misunderstood."

"Aren't we all. Come on, Lizzie, tell me what's what. I won't laugh. I won't cry. You're not like the others. You're not babbling, no rambling, no talking to unseen people. Completely rational as far as I can tell. So . . . ?"

"Hey, I'm not talking to unseen people *right now.* You learn some tricks after a few years. Don't talk to the invisible people while the visible people are looking."

"You're very funny."

"Look, I don't want to talk to you. I get enough of that from the doctors . . ."

"I told you; I don't have an M.D. or a Ph.D."

What are they teaching priests these days? This guy has no idea what charity work is all about. He's supposed to talk that baby-talk to me and send me down the hall to make wallets out of precut leather with the holes already punched so I won't hurt myself. He's supposed to come in with hand-me-down clothes and donated candy and stacks of old magazines that had the latest thing—from five years ago. He's supposed to tell me to trust him and then ask the nurse, in a frightened whisper, what's wrong with me. But he doesn't ask what's wrong with me. He asks, what's my story? My story.

"My trouble is, Father, that I'm an old soul in a young body, and I don't know what do about it and nobody else does either."

"That doesn't sound too bad."

I snort.

"There's more to it, I assume," he responds.

"My parents committed me after I told them I was reincarnated."

"That seems drastic. Reincarnation is not a new idea."

"Well, it wouldn't have been a big deal with them I guess, it would have been some kind of young girl rambling, I guess, if it hadn't been for the bleeding." I say this calmly, awaiting a reaction. I'm disappointed.

"Bleeding." He picks up a palm-size rock and cradles it gently, examining the veins and scars etched across its surface. "Blood is a powerful sign."

"To my father, it was a sign of insanity, especially since he thought I'd wounded myself."

"And you had not?"

"I had not." I push my sleeves up and thrust those telltale wrists under his nose. I'm getting a little tired of show-and-tell, but these days, I take my attention where I can get it.

"How did you get these?" he asks, putting the rock down on the ground and following the circular path of the real-flesh scars with his eyes.

"A legacy. Two lifetimes ago. I was a slave then."

"Can I?" He holds out his hands. I sigh, but place my arms in his palms. "Tell me," he demands, as he examines the scars.

The more I tell the tale, the more fantastic it sounds. The mysterious trunk, the quilt that evokes walking, talking memories and the lifetimes layered one on top of the other sound like some kid's fairy tale. But Father Tom listens earnestly, his expression changing from interest to fascination to outright horror. At the end, he grasps my hands. I scan his face, wondering if I will see the familiar, shocked revulsion I have seen so many times in my parents' eyes. But no, it's something else. Shock, yes. Not revulsion. Sympathetic horror and recognition.

He's silent for a long time, holding my hands. I begin to feel uncomfortable again.

"Years ago," he says finally, "a devoted monk named . . . well, I can't remember the name . . . became so fixated on the passion and crucifixion of Christ that he was stricken with wounds on his body that corresponded to the Savior's torture and death. It's called stigmata, child. That's what you have."

"You . . . it has a name?"

"Yes. Stigmata. I believe that's what you have. You hear about it happening in the Catholic Church. And often enough so that it's accepted as an authentic experience."

I look again at my wrists. Then I pull up the hem of my sweatpants and look at the ankle scars. I wasn't the only one.

"So, it *is* all in my mind," I murmur.

"No, no, Lizzie. Nothing is that simple. I think it's all in your mind in the sense that this person, this ancestor, is with you in some way, just as Christ was with the monk. The merging of spirits and all that. I don't know if that's reincarnation, or something else. In any case, no one considered the monk insane. He was practically considered a saint, a healer."

"A healer?"

"Yes."

"I'm marked."

"Maybe you're marked so you won't forget this time, so you will remember and move on. And Lizzie, I don't think you're meant to rot in a mental hospital."

"No," I whisper. "That wouldn't make sense. Certainly, Ayo

and Grace didn't go through what they did for that. What am I going to do?"

"I don't know, child." The priest smiles and pats my hands. "Listen, I will bring you some information on that monk, OK?" He shakes his head in wonder. "I feel honored to have met you, Elizabeth."

I stare at him. And I stare at my tortured flesh in his hands.

"Oh, that's a new feeling. Honored," I say. "Is this monk alive now?"

"Oh, no. That was some time ago." He lets go of my hands. "But his case is well documented with photographs."

"Wow."

When I tell Dr. Brun about stigmata, she isn't quite as impressed with the concept.

"Yesss . . ." she says, a week later in her office. She invites me to sit, but I can only pace. "I've heard of it. But stigmata is generally associated with devout religious persons."

"Generally doesn't mean always, does it?"

"Are you religious?"

I think about this for a moment before replying, "No, I just love God."

She smiles, smirks really. "I thought you told me your scars were from whips and chains," she says, raising an eyebrow.

"But it's the same MO as stigmata, you see. A mysterious physical trauma. I wasn't praying when it happened, though. I was remembering. Remembering something unbelievably traumatic."

"I'm not dismissing your theory, Elizabeth. I just . . ." She leans back and taps her desk with a pen. " . . . there are rare cases, but I don't think you fit the criteria."

"It really hurts me, Doctor, that you won't at least entertain the thought that this is an explanation for my condition," I say somewhat sarcastically.

"I'm sorry you feel that way, but I'm here to help you, not argue about nebulous theories."

"Does this mean my Christmas visit is canceled?"

"No, of course not."

Johnson Creek. The voices of Aunt Eva and Son Jackson drift in from the kitchen. A song. A hymn.

Son Jackson always comes for Christmas Eve dinner. He always brings bags full of fruit and nuts and Eva puts them in bowls on the dining room table. Now, as she takes the last pan of cornbread out of her oven, she joins the song he has started, soft and low and very, very old.

Even cocooned in Mary Nell's bedroom, with the door nearly shut, I hear them and I like the smile in Eva's voice. There with the late afternoon light sitting in my lap, I almost taste happiness; it laps around the edges of my memory, that feeling. It prods at me playfully, even as I think with dread of spending the next few days in front of my father's stare. I shouldn't mind him, but I still react to his silent, unintended intimidation. My parents' watchfulness has driven me to this quiet room, a small temple to Mary Nell, and into fleeting recollections that somehow make me hopeful.

Grace grew up in this house. Her father, a preacher of backwoods renown, presided over her wedding in Johnson Creek

Baptist Church across the road and afterwards they came back here and ate and danced in the backyard. The other preachers complained about that. Dancing and sinning, all one and the same. But I remember Grace's daddy—oh, it makes me smile to remember him laughing and whispering, "What a waste of good feet—they don't know what to do with what God gives 'em."

And Grace and George danced and danced until it was time to leave for their own house. Oh, her father always had a joke on his lips, unlike Dr. DuBose, who smiles and laughs, not when he wants to, but when it seems appropriate and correct. On holidays, not workdays.

It's good to remember the joy at that moment, because the bad time soon crowded out our smiles and songs. And one day, Grace left with her trunk for a trip that she hoped would help her come back to herself. But she never made it back.

"Stigmata? What?"

Daddy has a slice of pie on a plate in his lap, a napkin draped over one knee.

"That's the word the priest used." I keep my voice quiet, because Mother sometimes becomes upset if she thinks I'm getting overexcited. My little vacation has made her very nervous. She sits nearby on the porch steps, pretending that she's not listening.

"So, explain this to me," says my father. "This monk was so obsessed with the crucifixion that he crucified himself?"

"One way to look at it, I guess."

"Elizabeth," he says with an exasperated sigh, pulling at the neck of his turtleneck, "I want you to get well. I don't think that denial is the way to do that, do you?"

"Of course not, but that's what I mean. This isn't denial. The stigmata thing shows that there's a precedent, see? There's a word for what happened to me."

"Who are they letting into that place? Who is this guy? Is he recruiting for the church or something?"

He isn't listening. I lean back in the porch swing and the last of the sunlight leaves Johnson Creek.

Son Jackson comes out on the porch, still licking his teeth.

"Your Aunt Eva sho' can put it on the table," he says, sighing heavily.

"You helped, Mr. Jackson," says Mother. Son Jackson takes a seat next to my father, who glowers and shovels sweet potato pie down his throat. I worry that he might choke, but he just swallows hard.

"Yeah, well, I shoulda asked her to marry me long time ago," says Son Jackson, smiling rather gently.

"You did. I said no, remember?" Aunt Eva stands at the screen door. Son Jackson chuckles and she comes out to plop down on the swing with me. "I wonder will it ever get cold?" she says. "Christmas Eve and I'm sweating. Still, it's a nice night."

"Yeah, that's that crazy Alabama weather for you," says Mother.

"Stigmata," I continue, as if my father and I have never been interrupted, "is real, daddy. I believe Father Tom."

Daddy scowls. "That priest was giving you a story, Elizabeth, an interesting legend or something. It doesn't have a thing

to do with you. You marching with the saints now, girl? Those
doctors heard this stigmata story from you yet?" Daddy asks.
"What do they say?"

"They don't know what the fuck they're doing," I say, swinging my legs out and under the swing. Out and under. It begins
to rock, flying me and Eva past my mother's shocked face. Eva
smiles like a delighted child.

"Lizzie!" Mother clamps her hand over her mouth as if she
said the curse word. Eva looks at me from under her eyelashes.
Then she leans over and whispers, "Still making trouble I see,
Gracie." I start laughing and so does she; Son Jackson laughs
because Eva does.

"Is she one of you?" he asks her, pointing at me. Eva nods.
My parents look confused.

Jan. 5: "I hate to admit that this journal has helped me. I'm
probably too stubborn to tell Dr. Brun that since she gets on my
nerves so bad. But over the past couple of weeks, I've devel-
oped a need for the journal that wasn't there before. Damn that
Brun woman.

"I found myself strangely comforted by Aunt Eva; she called
me by her sister's name and for the first time I had confirmation
that Eva did understand, she knew who I was. In those moments when Ayo's and Grace's memories are chattering inside
my head, it's Grace that is the most emphatic. She—frightened,
alone in her strangeness—spent a lot of time moaning to herself, even after she left Johnson Creek for Detroit, then New
York. The first time Grace came back to me, her memories
spoke as one long moan inside my head."

I close the journal loudly. The world is a circle of light made by a bedside lamp and I'm lonely inside it. The silence outside the circle presses against the hospital walls. The journal eases my mental pain and illuminates it, makes everything swimming through my head touchable.

"**W**here is your mother?" Daddy bends over the
kitchen counter, his hands buried in a pan of raw chicken
parts. Through the open window, deep male voices argue.

"Listen up, brothers-in-law!" he yells into the backyard.
"That grill better be smoking when I'm ready to get out there!
Don't sit on the counter, Lizzie."

I jump down, careful not to spill my glass of lemonade.
Through the back-door screen, I see the twins, Phillip and
Frank, fiddling with the grill, while Ruth and Alene sit on the
grass shaking their heads, laughing. It seems strange to think of
seventy-year-old men as "the twins" but there they are, and
still arguing after all these years about the best way to tell when
the coals are ready. But as always, they are together.

I press my forehead against the metal screen. I wonder where those dolls are, those brown-skinned baby dolls Grace used to have sitting on her bed. Little boy dolls and a little girl doll. I try to remember where they are. Left them at home in New York. Left them behind for that trip to Montana.

Ruth catches my eye, sees me mooning. She lifts an eyebrow at me, motioning me outside. I take a seat next to her on the padded iron settee, noticing the drink in her hand. It wasn't lemonade.

"What's your problem?" she asks, following my eyes to where Alene and the twins stand around the flaming grill.

"I don't know. I wonder if all this agonizing over what Sarah knows or doesn't know about me is even necessary. Look at the twins. They survived fine without me."

"Survived, maybe. Thrived—well, I don't know. And Sarah's a whole different situation altogether. Little girls especially need their mothers."

"Yeah." I glance over just as Ruth takes a huge gulp from the glass and then sets it down on the patio table. I lift it, sniffing. "Gin? A little early, isn't it?"

"Yes, I believe it is." Ruth grins, snatching the glass back. "Don't nag. You don't want your man to see you nagging." She motions with her glass and I see Anthony Paul coming around the side of the house. He greets me with a kiss on the cheek, then whispers, "Are you all right?"

"I'll tell you later," I murmur.

"Tell me." Anthony Paul frowns at me, but I shake my head.

"I can't get into it now," I answer.

"Seems like you're already into it, whatever it is," he says as he takes my arm and strolls me over to the bench under the pecan tree. "You wanna give me a clue?"

Ruth joins the group at the grill.

"I've been trying to tell her," I say, letting my knees fold and settling on the wood bench. He scoots me over and sits down.

"Told who. What."

"Sarah."

"Your mother."

"Yes. Sometimes she looks at that quilt and I think she's getting it."

"*The* quilt?"

"Shh. No. Not the old quilt, a new one. I decided that the best way, the gentlest way, to reopen the subject of my past was to make this quilt. Kind of a story quilt. About Grace."

"Uh-oh."

"Yeah. Ruth says she knows, but she doesn't want to face it."

"I can certainly sympathize."

He leans his elbows on his knees, staring at the ground. Then he picks up one of last year's pecans and throws it across the back fence into Mr. McCracken's yard.

"I know," I say. "I don't know how to tell this story without freaking people out. Of course it sounds crazy. Of course they put me away. It sounds crazy." I put my hand on his knee. "But it feels real."

"What about the twins?"

"I don't know. I feel as though Sarah and I had the tighter connection. You know? Mother-daughter-mother. And she's still in a lot of pain from the past. I wanted to help her. But now. . . . To tell the truth, I'm afraid to take it any further. And I don't know if I'll ever tell the twins."

"I'm sorry."

"Thanks." I grab his hand and kiss it. "I want to resolve things with her before I go. But this all so hard."

"Before you go?" He's so surprised that I realize that I've forgotten to tell him about my plan to move to Atlanta and work with Ruth.

"Yeah. Um . . . I think it would be a good idea to get out of this cocoon, you know? Really start my life again. Ruth says she needs me to help her at the foundation."

"How come you haven't mentioned it before?"

"I don't know. I forgot that I hadn't. It doesn't mean," I add quickly as he straightens, looking stunned and hurt, "it doesn't mean that we can't keep . . ."

"It won't be the same. You know that. Oh, shit, why bother with this?"

"What?"

"Why bother with all this? You're making this too much work, Lizzie. I gotta deal with this reincarnation junk. That's keeping me up nights. On top of that, you're not even gonna be here! Do you even care?"

"Of course I do! I would never trust you with all of this if I didn't, you know that!"

"Stay with me, then. I know my place isn't much, but we can look for somewhere else."

"Anthony. It's not just my living arrangement that's getting old. It's my life. Literally. As long as I'm here, I'm in the past. Yes, it's a part of me. But I can't get stuck there."

"Why is everything so damned complicated with you?"

"It just is, Anthony."

We sit there. I hold his hand. Someone bursts out laughing

and I look up. Phillip and Frank demonstrate some old-as-hell dance step and Alene and Ruth try to join in.

"There's something I have to do here, Anthony. But after that, I can't stay." I smile and he squeezes my hand.

"Trying to get away from your past, huh? I guess that means me too. You said . . . you said I was part of your past."

"And my present. My today. I don't want to lose you."

"I ain't gonna lie, Liz. You might. You just might." He kisses me gently on the lips. "I'm gonna go. My parents are expecting me at their house."

I watch his long, lean frame leave.

"See you, son!" My father, backing out of the kitchen door with his large pan of long-marinated chicken carcasses, calls out to him. "Elizabeth, where's your mother?"

"I'll go look for her," I say. He nods and turns his attention to the twins, who are fiddling with the fire. "Get away from that grill, you two! As usual, I have to do all the work around here. Same thing, every Fourth."

I refill my glass with lemonade in the kitchen and take it with me into the dining room, through the living room and out into the hall.

"Mother! Daddy's putting the chicken on!"

There's silence except for the sound of footsteps above my head.

In the attic, she has laid the quilt full out on the floor. I'd left the red cloth for the binding on the table, but now Sarah holds it in her arms as she stands in the sunshine coming from the skylight, her head down. Even though I know the steps have been squeaking underneath my footsteps, she doesn't acknowledge my entrance. I don't know if she hears me. From behind her, I see the red cloth is looped over her arms, like a sash, like a gushing wound that she cradles close to her chest. She looks like she's been standing there forever.

I don't know what to do, but the ice-cold glass numbs my fingers and I look for a place to put it down, finally just bending and setting it on the floor.

The ice tinkles, and as I straighten, Sarah spins around, the red cloth whipping around her body. Her face is wet and wild. I've never seen her look so lost, my always so-correct mother. Was this how she looked all those years ago in Johnson Creek when one day she woke up bewildered and suddenly mother-less?

For a moment, I can't look into her eyes. She sobs quietly. I pick up the glass again, turning, thinking to escape down the stairs; I'm more of a coward than I thought.

"I came up," she says, "to cut the binding."

I stop and turn back to her.

"And I thought I would lay it all out, you know, to see how everything looked." She kneels next to the quilt. "I didn't realize until then . . . what a sad story it was."

"Yes," I say, coming closer. "I told you it was." I kneel too, on the other side. She won't take her eyes off me.

"Lizzie. You know this woman. You got the story . . . from her."

"Yes." I venture a glance at her face and the anguish I see there almost knocks me backward. But I straighten my spine and breathe deep.

For a moment there's only the sound of labored breathing in the attic and I watch the dust swirl around inside the sunbeams.

"So . . ." she says, her expression lightening a little, ". . . this person left her family and took a trip on a train to a city. She died near the mountains."

"Montana."

She shakes her head from side to side vigorously.

"Sarah . . . ?" I try to catch her eye but she won't look at me.

"I was standing there looking at it, the quilt, and I was thinking about Grace, you know. Thinking that those pictures on here look just like my mother's handiwork, you know. And then, I guess my mind started working overtime . . ."

"Sarah . . ." I wonder if she's noticed that I call her by her first name. She rambles like a runaway night train that had left the track and was shining its single beam of light into the unknown.

" . . . and I said to myself, 'Lizzie used to say those things, all those things back when she was in the hospital, about Grace and Bessie and all of that . . . goddamn reincarnation stuff.' The train and Detroit and New York and dying"—she sobs—"dying in some strange place. You know I've been really worried about that. Afraid. Afraid that you were getting sick again. Tell me, tell me you're not getting sick again . . ." She looks up at me hopefully.

I close my eyes and gather my fortitude. The moment is before us and I think about all I'm risking. But it's not like it was then. I'm strong and I know who I am. I know.

Sarah waits, looking as if she's drowning.

"I remember one time," I say quietly, dropping my eyes, "one Sunday after church, your daddy and I were getting ready to go fishing down to Mr. Poe's pond. You remember that pond where we always caught those big bream? I think it's dried up now . . ."

"It's been dry for years . . . since before you were b—" She stops, her eyes widening.

"Anyway, the twins were off playing baseball, but we couldn't find you and George was just about to go looking when you came running up from the creek. The bottom half of your dress was soaked and your feet. Your feet were caked with that wet mud. And you were carrying a syrup bucket filled with water and minnows." I smile. "I was just about ready to wale you for getting wet, but George, George he just very lightly put a hand on my arm and then picked you up, mud and all, and said, 'Now how did you know that's just what I was looking for, baby girl? Juicy ole minnows for my hook?' Then he gave me the bucket and swung you around until you laughed and laughed and then put you up on his shoulders. We caught the biggest fish that day."

"Who told you that? The twins?"

"They weren't there that day. They didn't get home until after dark. You were asleep by then. Did you tell them?"

"No . . . I'd forgotten about that . . . until now. Who told you?" Her face contorts into a dozen different expressions—grief, fear, disbelief, revelation.

"No one. I was there, Sarah."

"No, no . . ." She slumps forward, kneeling, pressing her head on the quilt, and I move towards her, crawling over the fabric to her.

"You probably have thought for all these long years that Grace—" I mentally shake myself "—that I left Johnson Creek because I was unhappy. But it wasn't that, baby. It was—fear. All these things were happening to me. Sarah—" I put my hands on her cheeks, lifting her head so that she'll look at me.

"The past was happening to me and I didn't understand it. I was afraid! I could have been committed." I laugh a little bitterly. "Hell, I was committed, just not until another lifetime."

"Why didn't you tell me?" she whispers in a raspy voice.

"I did, remember. Years ago."

"And I let you go. I let you leave me . . . again."

I move to embrace her. But we aren't ready to bake cookies together yet.

"No!" she yells, pulling away and standing up. "You're not my mother! Or—oh, God—my grandmother! That's insane. I'm sorry to use that word, but for God's sake, Lizzie! This is just the same thing all over again! I can't go through this again! I can't . . ."

I get slowly to my feet; I have no idea what to say next.

"This is crazy," Sarah whispers shakily, putting her hands up to her face.

"You know in your gut—in your heart—that I'm telling the truth." I take her hands down from her eyes. "You just don't want to think about it. It's too hard. I know it's hard. But I'm here. Ask me anything." I wipe the tears from Sarah's cheeks.

"I'm scared," she says faintly.

"OK. Of course. So am I, by the way." I lead her over to a chair and sit her down, still holding her hands. She slowly pulls them away and bends to take up the quilt.

"There's something else I need to put in there," I say, pointing to the quilt.

"What else is there?" Sarah asks. "It's almost finished."

"A link to the past," I answer, reaching under the table for the bag of scraps. "That's what this quilt is about. The past. And putting the past aside when we're through."

Her wide eyes never leave me as I root around in the bag. I find what I want and lay the tattered piece of blue cloth on the table. It's no more than two inches square, more or less, and so insubstantial it looks ready to dissolve into thin air.

"What is that?"

"It belonged to my mother," I say.

"It's not mine."

"No, Sarah. My mother." I speak very deliberately.

"Oh," she says, dropping her eyes. "Joy?"

"Well, yes. But I'm talking about my African mother. This was handed down, literally. It used to be a bigger piece. I was wearing something made from this, something my mother wove and dyed, the day they snatched me."

"They snatched you . . ."

"Slavers."

She makes a choking sound.

"Don't you remember? Joy's diary?"

"I tried to forget. I couldn't even look at that trunk after you . . . after you left. I just threw the quilt in there, blood and all, and took everything back to Eva." She purses her lips, picking up the fabric scrap and trying to smooth it out in her hand.

I take the cloth from her and scan the top of the quilt. Finally, I pin the blue piece around the neck of the Grace figure that was about to board the train; she looks as if she is wearing a scarf. There is silence as I find a needle and begin stitching it down. Sarah isn't looking at my fingers; her eyes are riveted on my face.

"If you are my mother," she says, "then tell me . . . about that day . . ."

"What day?"

"The day you left me," she snaps, her eyes hard.

I put down the needle and tell her. About the day before, with George taking his bath and me searching for my suitcase. About the memories I was having. About the pain.

She says nothing when I finish, just sits there with tears on her cheeks. Without wiping them away, she picks up the needle I had put down and finishes the stitching. The circle is complete and my daughter sits across from me with the gap finally closed.

"I used to beg God to send you back to me," she says trembling.

"I came as soon as I could."

The quilt slides to the floor as she puts her head in my lap. I stroke the hair out of her eyes.

July 23, 1900

Mama died in February. I could not make myself rite then. I don't know why Im riting now she aint around to holler rite daughter. It jest seem like I ought to see her story to the end. I knew her time was comin but when it happen it was like somebody knocking the breath out my chest. Somethin left here with her. I don't know. She was there drawin her last and she took my hand and laid it on the little baby quilt she don made. Take care of that little girl she say and she smiled and say I meant to put this in but I never did and she gave me a piece of blue cloth she had balled up in her hand. It was kinda raggedy but she open my hand and put it in and closed my fingers in a fist. Listen to your mama she say. I jest bow my head. Daughter she say I need some light. I got up to open the curtains and when I come back to the bed she gone.

I go to Mama grave and sat. I bring flowers and tell her bout the baby. Tell her bout Frank dancing in the yard he so happy. Tell her I gon be good a mama as she was to me. Tell her I miss her, but it aint so bad now that this child jumps for joy in my body.

March 1988—Birmingham

Father Tom compares mental hospitals to monasteries. Separation from the world at large allows quiet contemplation, he once told me. The price of this, of course, is the physical and mental poking and prodding, but he's right. Most of the time you're alone or with people who are so far away, you might as well be alone. It's easy to hide.

I ask to be in the art class. My sketchbooks and journals overflow with past-life episodes. My new therapist loves them but doesn't believe a thing I tell him.

"True faith is belief in the midst of unrelenting pressure," Father Tom wrote to me. "You are clearing a path to your place among the saints."

That's a little too much for me. I don't feel holy at all. Just annoyed.

I choose a sketch for my first attempt at painting. The teacher is a very old white man who comes in from a nearby retirement home. His therapy is to direct ours. He isn't a bad teacher. He's patient in a way that a younger person wouldn't be, and I find myself relaxing and letting my fingers move the way they want.

Maria Elena is in the class. Maria Elena, a woman of about forty or so, swallows things, and I'm surprised that she's allowed to mess with paints. The first time I glance at her, she smiles and waves with her brush. I frown at her, because we're supposed to be just at the sketching stage. And sure enough, the next time I look there's red paint smeared around her mouth and on her hands and she's slippery and happy. I start laughing and the teacher, a Mr. Hart, follows my eyes and sees her, lets out a yelp and runs to call someone.

When he leaves I go over and stand next to her. She's turned the little pot of paint over in her lap and everything, her hands, her dress, the floor beneath her stool, is crimson wet.

"Why do you do that?" I ask.

"Because I'm hungry," she says immediately, licking the tips of her fingers. "Haven't you ever been hungry?"

Well, yeah.

She gets up from the stool and starts across the room, dragging a path of paint behind her. Two nurse's aides run up to lead her to where she's already going: the bathroom, to wash it all off.

The paint stains Maria Elena's stool and the floor around it. Mr. Hart comes hurrying back.

"Well, let's all get back to our work," he says, looking rather pointedly at me. I look at the red paint.

"Someone will be around to clean that up, shortly," he added.

I go back to my seat and begin erasing the sketch I've begun and start another. Mr. Hart's voice is a background hum, and an old conversation drifts by.

"So," says Grace to Martin one day as they lie in bed high above the Harlem street, "we were there at the rail. And they brought somebody. A boy."

I pick up some paint on the brush.

"They take him and haul up, and it's funny, Martin, it look almost like they was cradling him, you know. Holding him like a baby. He was so weak, he could have been a baby."

On the white-primed canvas, I draw a swirl of red, a hurricane with a small dark eye, a doorway.

"And he didn't scream. He didn't even whimper. He just looked up at the sky as if he were giving a prayer of thanks. And then . . . then they just hung him over the side of the boat and let him go."

A dark, naked shape drifts toward the vortex. The red spiral moves, rises to meet it. Small legs and arms fly out in a confused jumble, needing something solid but finding nothing to cling to.

Grace stirred in Martin's arms. Outside, the sound of a car screaming to a stop made her jump a little, but didn't break the spell. He stared at her glazed eyes, knowing she was somewhere he couldn't reach. "I watched him fall. He was so graceful. He flew, Martin. As I watched, he looked at me, inviting like. I wanted to go. I wanted to go down there with him through the doorway to heaven."

"That's not your original idea, Miss DuBose, but very . . . compelling." Mr. Hart stands behind me, his chin almost on my shoulder, considering the spare shapes on my canvas.

"Some background, maybe. A few more secondary subjects in the painting for perspective. I see a story there, but it's all alone. Embellish!"

He moves away, and I take up another brush to paint a gray ship and a brown girl standing at the rail.